You'd Better
Believe It

Detective Chief Superintendent Colin Harpur novels
by Bill James:

You'd Better Believe It
The Lolita Man

Bill James

You'd Better Believe It

A Foul Play Press Book

The Countryman Press
Woodstock, Vermont

You'd Better
Believe It

1

He was shopping for another marksman, someone for that nice, comfortable, fourth seat in the back of his car, someone who would also stay close and do a tidy job when they were out of the car and sprinting towards a double barrel. It would be soon: the word was about. Harpur could be choosy. Wasn't it a privilege to work with him and get shot at with him? Police boredom was beautiful. Men offered themselves for tricky outings to break the dullness.

A few people, some of them sharp, said he ought to think about Brian Avery, so he thought about him. Avery was a promising cop, and Mrs Avery had promise too. These team things could push you into contact with a man's wife and family. A good team grew very close, met in one another's houses not just the nick, did a lot of their drinking together, and brought their women to some sessions. He would be glad of a route to Mrs Avery, and if he picked Brian it would be there. Avery had commendations, one or two of them very strong stuff. His shooting was tournament standard, at least with pistols. He looked right – alert, nimble, solid, big but not so fleshy big that as soon as he turned up anywhere in a suit people asked his number. Alert? Alert, or edgy? Avery was on the short list so Harpur had watched him the last couple of days in the club bar and still couldn't make up his mind whether what glinted there added up to brightness or panic. The dossier had nothing to show he might crack. The folk Harpur talked to had worked with Avery or had had him under their orders, and they all admired the man and trusted him, said he had a future. Wasn't it all irresistible?

Harpur arranged to do some shooting on the range when Avery was there, though not to see whether he could hit bull's-eyes. Harpur knew the answer to that: Avery had prizes. But Harpur needed to see that he took care. Since the shooting of Steven Waldorf, the world was ready to drop like ten tons of newsprint on any error with a gun by British policemen.

Prone and standing, Harpur shot well this morning with the .38, fifteen out of seventeen and fourteen out of seventeen. Avery who came after him had a maximum on each with the .38, and then did it with a .45. The new firearms sensitivity had brought an extension to the range, imported from the States, and Harpur went there next, the .38 in his hand. It always made him think of one of those grottoes for kids at Christmas in big toy departments. You walked a mock-up London street, with plywood façades of corner shops, warehouses, a pub, a filling station. It looked like somewhere in dockland. As you trod the timed route, dummy figures swung up suddenly at spots in the urban battleground and threatened you – or didn't. The test was to identify the figure fast and fire or hold your fire, whichever was right. One figure had a shotgun, another an Armalite. They could pop up anywhere, like in life itself, and you ought to have a shot, or two shots, smack into their dotted-line hearts within a couple of seconds. No need to shout the rigmarole warning; that was deemed to have been given earlier. Speed was the thing, controlled speed. A woman carrying a baby, a police sergeant in uniform, and a milkman on his rounds could also jump into view, and it was considered poor form to drill any of these, especially the baby. For one shot in a good soul you lost points, and for two your whole score disappeared. Return to Go, do not collect £200. That was for the British – in the States they probably just docked you a half for a chamberful in any of them, baby included.

Harpur went through pretty quickly today. He had done it five times before and although they shuffled the locations for these enemies, friends, and innocents, he felt on top of things, swift to the kill, though not too swift. And he did knock over the villains in good time with shots that were not all in the heart but spread over a decent rectangle between neck and navel. The pity was that he also shot the sergeant, a bullet very high in

6

the right shoulder, almost a miss because at the moment he fired he knew he had it wrong and tried to swing the pistol up and away. After the penalty, he came out at eleven from a possible fifteen; poorish. It was not the first time he had shot the wooden sergeant. 'He after your job, sir?' the inspector who did the scores asked. Harpur watched Avery do another perfect round in two seconds less than his own.

In the afternoon he sent for Avery. 'I'm getting together a group for a job that could be coming up, Brian.'

'I thought you'd never ask, sir.'

A couple of nights later they all assembled in Harpur's house with their women, and Megan did some food and helped keep the talk easy and general. This was social only, a dose of *esprit de corps*, not tactical planning. The women would not be in on that. He was able to talk a little with Ruth Avery, nothing rushed, nothing noticeable. She said Brian was grateful to have been chosen, and seemed to share the excitement. That would do as a start. He spoke well of Brian, but not so well that she might come to think he was the only man worth talking about. She was smart, a little heavy, cheerful-looking and about five years younger than Harpur, the kind of brassy girl he occasionally found himself gazing at with appetite these days. Appetite he did not signal tonight in the presence of spouses.

2

Briefings – Christ, what a laugh! Sketch maps, photos, coloured chalk, so picturesque. And the chat that went with them, calm and organized to make things sound all buttoned up. On the job, though, there could be fright, collapse, those unaccountable sudden dives into stupidity. Listening to briefings or giving them himself, Harpur occasionally wanted to slink from the room and find something real. He never did. These lecturettes had to be done because the geography of a street and the geography of a face might be vital. Just the same, boredom doused him like a bucket of slops as soon as a session began. Talky, talky. Now, he brought his own talking to an end, turned away from the blackboard and sat down. 'One thing more. Eight of us will be armed, standard issue .38s.' For what followed he tried to eliminate all mockery from his voice. 'I remind you that handguns will be drawn from the holster only if you believe, and reasonably believe, your life is threatened. In this event, you are to shout a warning, "Armed police", if possible more than once. If you fire, it will be at one of the specified targets, not at the tyres of vehicles or anything else. There have been recent accidents. You may have heard.'

Morning sun, mild and kindly, glazed the leaves of street beeches and made film titles over the ABC shimmer winningly, *Plague, Children For Sale, Don't Forget The Foreplay.*

'All little known early works of D. W. Griffith,' Leo Peters said.

Two huge seagulls patrolled Woolworth's parapet, screeching now and then across the rattle of traffic. A good-natured breeze nudged the beech branches and their shadows swirled and eddied on the pavement – a delightful sight, Harpur thought. Delightful? Who was he, for God's sake, Cecil Beaton?

Behind him in the unmarked Granada, Leo Peters hummed a fine tune. Alongside Leo, Brian Avery chewed gum. It sounded a bit too fast. Next to Harpur, Chris, the driver, also chewed but without the rush. 'What's the song, Leo?' Chris asked.

Leo moved from humming into words and sang: *'That we may build from age to age an undefiled heritage.'*

'Some chance,' Chris said.

'It's "Land of our birth we pledge to thee",' Leo told him.

The driver seemed to see something and his hand moved to the starter. Except for Avery's chewing, even faster now, they all grew silent. 'No, not them,' Chris said, and his hand went back to the wheel.

Over the ABC thin, very white cloud stretched across the bright blue of the June sky like an unrolled bandage. One of the gulls sidled urgently along the parapet, cried once more, its body taut, and then in a great gleam of white spread its wings and flew down the street and away.

'I think its proper title is "The Children's Song",' Leo said, humming again.

'Who cares?' Avery muttered.

Leo recited: '*Land of our birth, our faith, our pride, For whose dear sake our fathers died; O Motherland, we pledge to thee – Di da di da di da di da.*'

'*Head, heart and hand, through the years to be,*' Harpur said. 'Did that at school.'

'That's it, sir,' Leo exclaimed.

Avery said, 'Jesus, I'm getting jumpy; I mean, not knowing whether they'll show. Only the waiting.'

'You don't look a bit jumpy,' Harpur said, turning. 'Like a rock.'

'Yes,' Chris said, 'calm as the doldrums. I don't know how you do it.'

'Only five of the sods, Brian,' Harpur told him. 'I've got twenty good lads spread around here, including the other sharpshooters. And more units on call.'

Chris tensed again, and leaned towards the starter, and again did not complete the move. 'It's me who's jumpy.'

A couple of girls on a day off sauntered towards the shops and paused near the Granada, obscuring Harpur's view of the bank. The girls bent to look in.

'Wow,' Harpur murmured.

'I know one of them.' Leo sounded apologetic. The girls smiled.

'Nice,' Harpur commented. 'Both. This town has the best.'

'Get them away from here, for God's sake,' Avery said. 'It's time.'

'Not quite,' Chris told him. 'No harm.'

Peters wound down the rear window.

'After pick-ups as usual, Leo?' one of the girls asked.

'Melanie, you're looking great.'

9

'You working or something, Leo?'

'Sort of, yes.'

'What the fuck does she think?' Avery gabbled it, needing to chew even as he spoke, but the girl caught his tone and looked troubled.

'Cheery fellow you got there, Leo.'

'Summer sales, ladies?' Harpur asked. He shifted slightly so as see Lloyd's again.

'Oh, who's your interesting friend, Leo?' the other girl said, glancing at Harpur.

'Look, push off girls, will you?' Avery said.

He could be right about himself: a lot of men who were top warriors once things had started could not put up with waiting. In a few minutes Avery would be somebody different. Harpur was sure of it.

'I'll see you some time. I'll call you,' Peters told the girl.

'I bet!'

'I will.'

'Christ, he will,' Brian Avery said. 'Now get lost.'

'See you, girls,' Harpur called. 'Well it ought to be getting close.' His information went only so far. Of course. It said the number of men, and named four of them, it said the time. It did not say what vehicle or vehicles to look for. It said armament, but not what kind. You had to expect shotguns on this sort of job, though. Information might be right when it started but could turn wrong because people changed their plans. Leaks could go two ways. 'We'll give it an hour.'

'They'll all be at home in Peckham having a giggle,' Avery said, 'thinking of us sitting here sweating.'

'Could be,' Harpur replied.

'Not that I'm sweating.'

'Me, yes, a bit. Sorry men,' Peters said.

'Your nark, sir – is he . . .?' Avery began.

'Solid.' Jack Lamb had never been wrong, or never as wrong as this. Harpur knew no grass to come near him. He and Jack Lamb: it was a partnership, risky, secret, close, that ancient replica of a marriage of convenience, a cop and his tipster.

'Can we risk the radio?' Peters asked. 'Let the others know

we're sitting tight, never mind the time, and they're to do the same?'

'Best not.' In fact he waited above an hour. Towards the end, Brian Avery's chewing grew almost relaxed. Nothing was going to happen today. Harpur broke the silence and told the other cars it was a dud. *'Mea culpa*, lads.'

'You what?' Chris asked.

'Pity. I was looking forward to it,' Avery remarked, as the Granada made for the nick. 'Kick your nark's arse, sir, if he hasn't scarpered. Promising us a nice caper like that. Hope you didn't give him anything in advance. But maybe it's only a postponement. We might get another go at the bastards.'

'They'll come.'

3

Jack Lamb made no contact for more than a fortnight. When he did, his voice on the phone was as big and cheerful and matey as ever. People thought of narks as small, slippery sods, whispering their inside stuff. They ought to see Jack. As ever, also, Harpur listened, saying nothing much, waiting for Jack to give time and place. It could all have been done on the phone but Jack liked a touch of face to face and feared leaks in British Telecom, anyway. You did not push or badger or dictate to a nark: it was *his* eyes or skin or kids that were at risk. Remember Toothpick Charlie in *Some Like It Hot*. Jack said there was an auction, antiques and jewellery, where he had some items for sale and wanted to keep an eye on the bidding. Would Harpur like to meet him there?

God. 'Sounds pleasant,' Harpur replied.

'Pieces that have been in the family for years. I feel it's a good time to realize, Col.'

'You know about these things.'

'I wouldn't want you uneasy about where they come from, that's all. Not ... not embarrassed.'

'Good Lord, no.' Narks meant uneasiness. They went their way and you shut your eyes, for as long as they talked good tips to you. Always you worried whether you were giving more than you got. Always you wondered whether those above might suddenly decide you were an accessory, not just an ear.

'You had a bit of a wait at the bank, I hear?' Lamb laughed noisily.

'It was a beautiful morning. Gets us out of the office. I wouldn't have you blame yourself.'

'I'd have called earlier, but I'm pretty occupied. Fascinating deals.'

All Jack's deals were worrying, and fascinating ones were a hell of a prospect.

Jack arrived late at the auction with a woman older than himself in tow, nearly as big and nearly as beautifully dressed, both of them full of smiles and mystery. They sat down, the woman smelling of some good perfume and wine. She held out a thick hand decorated with a diamond-cluster ring. 'Oh, a towering day,' she said. 'But isn't it always, with Jack? I'm Fay Corby.'

Jack leaned across her. 'They'll come again, Col. I've got the lot.'

'What went wrong last time, Jack?'

Fay held a burly finger to Harpur's lips. 'Are these your nothings, Jackie?' The auctioneer announced some bracelets, rings, clasps and necklaces.

He nodded and grew solemn. 'I'm attached to these, you know, Fay. A shame to see them go.' Again he leaned towards Harpur. 'They've been in the family for so long, Col, but there comes a time.'

'You said.'

'Did I?'

None of the descriptions Harpur heard from the auctioneer, none of the views he was given now of articles sold, recalled anything on current lists of missing property. Jack would not put crazy strains on their liaison, surely to God? Two brooches made more than £4,000 each and Jack grew less affected by grief. They left Fay to watch the rest placed. In the public bar next door Jack, big as a cliff and supple in his grand summer suit, caused silence as they entered. They stood at the bar with vodkas, two tall, weighty men but Harpur looking like a minia-turization. 'The other day Col – late intelligence came their way. Enough to cause postponement. Only that.'

'Intelligence? That we were waiting for them?'

Lamb pushed his great heaped dinner-plate of a face near Harpur's. 'You're not saying I leak from both ends are you, Col?'

'What late intelligence, Jack? What did they know? How?'

'These boys are organized. They'll go through with it. You must be waiting again.'

'What did they know, Jack? How?'

'Look, it reached them that only half the due loot would be there. Their first tip said six hundred grand, which was right. But some switch of bank storage, and it comes down with a bang to a quarter of a million, even less. Maybe not much more than a hundred thousand. Not worth the petrol. They've got a nice mouth in the bank, high up.'

Lamb waved to someone across the bar. Show off your tame cop, it could pay in all sorts of ways. People liked dealing with protected businesses. And, something else – once in a while a clued-up nark made his policeman look as if he might be on the take. He took him where the smell of loot was in the air – say, a jewellery auction – and made sure the officer was seen. Never mind whether the cop did or didn't take ... how would it sound to a jury? So, if one day a detective wanted to break the partnership, turn religious on his nark, withdraw protection, the nark might need to issue a threat or two. Any tipster who could make his cop look like a partner had a guarantee of con-tinuing friendship and sweet, thoughtful treatment. It wasn't only the police who could fit someone up. Harpur knew all these things, saw the ploys, and sometimes had a laugh with Jack about the refinements of grassing. Narks meant more than uneasiness, they were peril. Every copper knew it, includ-ing a bevy doing time. Juries were poor at understanding how 'information received' was received. They grew nervy and un-pleasant about the bargains, the blind eyes, the hobnobbing of cops and villains, and they did not admire or trust officers who drank with crooks, especially crooks who put jewels up for auction and dressed sharper than Giscard.

'Is there a date for the re-run, Jack?'

'Not yet.'

God, it was just one of those useless general chit-chats that Jack seemed to like so much.

'I can tell you this,' Lamb said. 'It's bigger than last time, big bigger. There's going to be a day when there's four million plus in the bank. They'll get the word.'

'Do we get it?'

'I'll get it. I think so.'

'Christ, you must. If we ask Lloyd's—'

'They'll hear and cancel. Of course, I'll get it.'

'How many men?'

'Same. Five. They'll take what's carry-able.'

'Holly, Gordon, Mann, Morgan and who else?'

'Still haven't got the fifth. A nobody. Probably the driver. Could be local – knows the roads.'

'Weapons?'

'Yes. Don't know what this time, either. Expect the worst.'

'Vehicles?'

'Oh, come on, you're supposed to be a whiz-kid. Cars to be stolen the night before . . . who knows what they'll be? Not old bangers. Will you be waiting for them?'

'I believe you, Jack.'

'I should bloody hope so. Col, you ever handled anything like this before, excuse me asking?'

'A bank job with guns? To meet them head on? Not for a while.'

'Can you handle it?'

Harpur thought about this. 'Who knows? I'm a first-class shot. So's Leo. But that's on the range. You're asking, could I fire to kill a man? I'll let you know. I've got another tidy boy with a gun now, called Brian Avery.'

'I heard.'

'What did you hear?'

'That you'd taken him on.'

'What else? That's he's a wanker?'

'Some say so. I've got no evidence.'

'His record is golden.'

'There you are then. It must be OK. Nice wife.'

'I heard.'

'All this bloody fret about guns in the police. With lads like Holly you don't hang about, you know. None of that "Armed police, stop!" crap. Bang, bang first, or else. Let them work it out that you're armed when lead starts ripping the boiler-suits.'

'We'll manage.'

'I worry about you. Once, Holly did me the deepest damage. Why else would I be shopping him? But you boys mustn't let that mistake over Waldorf and David Martin shake you.'

'As I said, we'll manage.'

Harpur did not return with Jack to the auction room. Later that day he had another nark to see, a nark who looked like a nark except that he was black, no plentiful species. Royston Marlborough Paine was smaller than Lamb, not as rich, nor as useful, in more danger. He regularly came up with a rich crop of piss-poor tips about small-time villains and tiny-tot crimes, to divert attention from some of the big things he knew about and kept dark, an old and famous dodge. But one day there might be something real. They met in the cargo-lift of the hospital where Paine worked as a porter. At night it was not used, but during the day it brought down crates of foul linen, maybe limbs for the burner, and Harpur tried not to breathe in more than he had to. Paine could fix the controls so that they went up non-stop six floors, then down again, and back up if he had a lot to say. Generally he did, a fat gabble of bugger-all. Harpur would leave the basement swearing never to keep the rendezvous again. He always did. Paine was a habit.

'You know a man called Darch?' Royston asked tonight, as they soared. The reek of ganja filled the lift, beat back the hospital's antiseptic.

'Black?'

'No, man. You think I know only blacks?'

'Darch. Petty thieving?'

'Could be.'

'Dick Darch?' Another nobody. Harpur would get out first time they returned to ground. This nobody might even be inside.

'The one,' Paine said. 'Just out of Maidstone.'

'A loser.'

'Him into something big and juicy.'

'Yes?'

'You don't believe?'

'I hear you talking to me.' 'Big' for Paine might mean doing two electric meters instead of one. They were at the top. The doors opened and he heard groaning from a ward. The steel slid back and they descended. 'When?'

'I don't hear no date, just that it's a real big pay-day for them.' Paine stared at him. 'Someone else told you something like this? A special day.'

'Where?'

'I don't know. And I don't know what it is, neither. We go up again?'

'What else? Darch in something big?'

'Dick can drive, you know. I mean drive. Rallies. He been telling friends him due for big driving that special day. But no rallies due, that I heard about. Darch hoping for a Volvo, but can't be sure. Says a Volvo can bust out of trouble, bumpers like a oak tree.'

'Have you heard Darch talking yourself?'

'Not me. No tracing, man. Roundabout.'

'Good. Take plenty of care.'

'And you, Mr Harpur. Don't you finish up in here. Or the other place. You all right with a piece?'

'We manage.'

'Big boys don't stop to talk. Shoot second no good.'

'I'll get out now, Royston. Be in touch. I might owe you.'

'You will, Mr Harpur. You do, Mr Harpur.'

He stepped into the basement and the doors shut behind him. Long tunnels stretched in three directions under the hospital, well-lit but deserted now – Harry Lime territory without the rats and shit. There would be more freight lifts and a criss-cross of routes where plumbers and electricians messed about with drains and conduits in the ceiling, and along which bodies went discreetly to the morgue and tissue to the incinerator. In the day it might be busy with all sorts. At night a man could be cornered and very conveniently and discreetly seen to. He hoped Paine never left the hospital this way at night. Narks ought to keep clear of tunnels and basements and shadowed alcoves. In a warren like this, a man could find his exits netted up and something final at his throat. A hospital was no place to die under.

4

Harpur's next chance to speak to Mrs Avery came during a parent-teacher evening at the John Locke Comprehensive. There had been no more information, so pressure was off and he could take a bit of time for family duties. Megan and he were strong on the school and community, especially Megan who followed her parents, Highgate doctors with caring souls and a belief that the masses would respond to education. John Locke needed all the help it could get and for the sake of his two daughters, if nothing else, Harpur did what he could, within limits. The school had wanted him to be a governor but, although the police would have approved this sign of social commitment, he drew back. His daughters would have hated it. They already had a rough enough time at the school because he was a cop. In any case, to go in so deep could become a tedious nuisance.

Brian Avery was working tonight and Ruth had come alone. While Megan queued to see their daughters' physics teacher, Harpur bumped into Mrs Avery in the English Literature area. Spotting Harpur she hung back to talk, although she had already finished her session with the teachers there. She had dressed up this evening, as if a mother had to put on a tip-top show for the sake of her children, even at a place like John Locke. The yellow cotton suit seemed to take half a stone off her, not that Harpur was bothered about weight. These days he kept a look out for expansiveness, hoping it might mean jollity. Jollity they seemed short of at home. For a little while they discussed the school and kids, while with part of his mind he followed a conversation nearby between a young woman teacher and a middle-aged West African couple Harpur knew well, about how best to help their son at home studying *The Importance of Being Earnest*. 'Lascelles told me that when she says, "The line is immaterial," this is a joke, for laughter,' the mother said.

'It used to be a comedy, yes,' the teacher replied. 'Things have changed.'

Out of nowhere, it seemed, Ruth Avery suddenly asked, 'Is it all right with Brian? He's scared you might cut him out of your group. Mr Harpur, it's dragging him down. There's been a change in him. It's bad.'

'Good Lord. Throw him out? Why should he think that?'

She was watching his face very carefully to plumb beneath the words, like a detective interrogating. 'I don't know. It's an idea he's picked up from the way you talk to him, or maybe from how you look at him. He's sharp.'

Yes, he must be, if he had sensed Harpur's shadowy doubts. 'But he's everything I was looking for.'

'What I tell him. He's never let anyone down yet.' She regretted that last word and repeated the sentence without it. 'He's never let anyone down. Never would.'

'His record is out of this world and – '

'Do you like him, Mr Harpur?'

'He's fine. A first-class officer.' It seemed the wrong setting to make a move – a woman full of worry for her husband – but he said, 'Look, Ruth, I have to press on here now. Suppose I give you a call one day soon? I can put your mind at rest.'

He saw her flush slightly. Did she spot that the conversation had abruptly changed its nature? After a small hesitation she replied, 'All right. I suppose you know when he won't be at home.'

'I can find out, yes.'

'What I mean – I wouldn't like him to know I'd been discussing his problems with you,' she said hurriedly.

'That's wise.' He went to talk to the teacher. As they came at John Locke, this man did not seem too bad. Even in a time of cut-backs and joblessness, the brightest and best would not rush to posts at this school. Once or twice Harpur had thought of sending the girls away to board, or at least transferring them to a private place in the town. They had squashed the idea.

The West Indian couple was waiting for him. 'Mr Harpur, I've been talking to the art teacher. Wouldn't you say that's a great subject? You heard of any great black artists, Mr Harpur? That's a field wide, wide open and my boy got talent. I like that idea – a studio, smocks. There's a road to freedom, now. Don't matter how an artist talks, don't matter about colour, except in the picture.'

'A good life.'

'But your girls, Mr Harpur?'

Whitey ought to know how to get the best out of British schooling, because hadn't Whitey been through it and landed himself a fair job?

'Science. Nursing. Free uniform.'

He liked that, and had a laugh. 'Oh, yes, Mr Harpur. You got one yourself in the cupboard.'

Later he met up with Ruth Avery again, this time in Domestic Science. Megan was close by, looking at a new oven, and Mrs Avery spoke very quickly and quietly, as if she and Harpur already had some kind of private understanding, but it was still all about her husband. 'I'm scared he'll do something stupid – he's so keen to impress.'

'What sort of thing?'

'Oh, I don't know, but he seems to be into some secret investigations of his own. Perhaps they're not secret, though. Possibly you've put him on to them?'

'Where? What investigations?'

'So he's not under orders.'

'Not mine, but it could be that – '

'No. This is something he has concocted himself, I know. I shouldn't have mentioned it. Please don't let him know. Please.'

Megan returned and they had to talk about Prize Day and the mini-bus fund. A comforting smell of pastry reached them, but did not relieve the new anxieties Ruth Avery had handed to Harpur.

5

There was an interview with Barton, the Chief Constable, and Iles, his Deputy. 'Just for a progress report,' Iles said, fixing the time on the phone.

'None yet,' Harpur told him.

'Well, we can get in nice and early,' Iles said.

They met in the Deputy's room, not Barton's. The Chief seemed to think this lent informality. 'I don't want you to feel I'm breathing down your neck, Colin.' Barton had arranged for his voice to be bright and friendly, at least to begin with. It changed after a while. 'I've got to tell you, I'm not happy about Lloyd's. There's bound to be gun-slinging, isn't there? If things turn out badly for us – I mean some bystander getting shot – I'm going to be asked why I didn't just stop it happening by making it plain in good time that we know what's due to occur. Bloody MPs and farts from the Homo Office will scream that I connived at a shoot-out.'

'We can take some very big people here, sir,' Harpur replied.

'This would be Holly, Mann, Gordon and Morgan?' Iles asked.

'Holly would be a catch, no question,' the Chief admitted. 'And Mann. But the bloody Homos don't like salvoes on the street, post you-know-what in London. We're inviting it, aren't we? Do correct me if I'm wrong.'

Grey, sly, long-faced, Barton was going out of the job in eighteen months and had taken to ostentatious and phoney politeness lately, ready for seeking something in business. He had hoped to coast this last stretch of his service, breathing in only stately valedictions and the kindly fumes of all-night special piss-ups. Lloyd's on his plate at this time was unfair, a big and pestilential lumber.

Iles said, 'And we're still without a date, aren't we?'

'That will come, sir. These villains haven't made their own decision yet. They are waiting for certain information.'

'You're going entirely on nark intelligence, yes?' Iles asked. He was grey, too, though only just into his forties, bony-faced, soft-voiced, small-mouthed, beautifully shaved. He had come from another force three months before and Harpur knew little about him; a mistake. On the face of it he seemed straightish, politic and easy to dislike.

'Yes, I'm working from my informants at this stage,' Harpur said.

'They'll move when the bank is stuffed super-full, isn't that it?' Barton continued. 'But we can't ask the bank when that'll be, because there's a leak at the top, right?'

'It would blow the whole thing, sir.' Harpur wished immediately that he had not said this. Barton might choose to play it like that for the sake of safety and a quiet life.

'Have we done anything about the bank voice?' Iles asked.

'Not yet, sir. For the same reason – any move that way, and the ripples reach London at once and the job is off.'

'So we're standing by while a high bank official betrays his employers,' Barton said.

Seeing the operation near death, Harpur said hurriedly to the Chief, 'These big-time London bastards popping down the motorway to clean up in one of our towns – I think we've got to show them we're not here for the taking, sir. They consider us a bunch of nothing dumbos, just here to provide them pickings. It's a pattern all over the country. Day-trips. Dirtying our ground, these sods from the Smoke.'

Barton's face twitched. After some sort of failure years ago in London he hated all things metropolitan, especially the

21

police, and Harpur knew it. 'Damn, I would like to pull in Holly,' the Chief said. 'Those prancing Yard twats with their leather-coated canes haven't been able to nail him, not for a decade. More.'

'He's made a fortune, and a fool of them, sir.' Harpur piled it on.

Sharp as a good Deputy should be, Iles picked up Barton's changing attitude. 'It would be quite a last act for you, sir.'

A knighthood, after all this time?

'Just keep me informed, in real detail, how you mean to organize this, Colin,' Barton said. 'We'll let it run as it is, for a while at any rate.'

Harpur reached for his briefcase. 'I can show you most of it now, sir – disposition of men, vehicles, support groups.' He decided not to mention weapons. Barton had been steered through the shoals into optimism; why scupper him now?

'Yes, let's see,' the Chief said, eyes cheery for a moment in the worry-gut face.

'This will parcel the buggers up,' chortled Iles.

6

He rode the hospital lift again at night with Royston Paine. Between the basement and cardiology, twenty in fives passed. Risk capital. Royston might be improving. It no longer seemed beyond belief that he would ever come up with something. Paine shoved the notes into the pocket of his glistening white coat as if they were Kleenex, and did a small shuffle that could mean excitement or rage that there was no more. He had a trolley of books with him for distribution in the wards.

'Heard any more about Darch, Royston? Any date, time, place?' Just little matters of exactitude that he could have ready when next Barton and Iles switched the grill on.

'Nothing like that, Mr Harpur. I mean, not yet. But he still behaving big. He got something very good coming, I know it.'

They began descending.

'I heard we got a stranger around,' Paine said. 'A big boy from up the motorway.'

'What sort of big boy?'

'Smart, you know. Big.'

'Alone.'

'Looks like that.' Paine picked a book from the trolley. 'You know this story, Mr Harpur? *The Masters* by Charles Percy Snow?'

'I think so. Look, is this to do with the stranger?'

'No, man.' He laughed in a big, tickled, black way. 'How would it be to do with that? Just conversation, you know. This book is about Cantab.'

'Cambridge, yes.'

'I think some call it Cantab. This book is about who will be in charge of Christ's College. They got Jesus College, Trinity College, too. Any God College?'

'Who's the fucking stranger around, Royston? What does it mean?'

'I got no name, but his suits are pretty, I heard. This boy is a somebody, or a somebody's assistant. In the Four Horsemen and Alfredo's, asking things, like he was getting the picture on this town ready for something. They sends one man ahead sometimes. This could be a very high-class outfit. Some chicken-shit nobodies living up the Ernest Bevin estate are showing him around. You know what sort – steal from a kid. Michael Martin Allen, he one.'

'So I need to know about the visitor, Royston.'

'Young, I hear. Not thirty. Maybe no form.'

'Tall, short, dark, fair?'

'I can't ask a lot of questions, Mr Harpur. I listen.'

'You haven't seen him yourself?' It was turning out a real Royston special.

'I will. But I'm telling you now what I hear.'

'What's the bloody use of –' But at the basement Harpur did not attempt to leave. They climbed again. 'How long has he been here?'

'Couple of days.'

'Do you know where he goes?'

'The clubs, like I said, with Michael Martin Allen, maybe others.'

'No, in the day. You said casing the town. Which part?'

'In the day? No, I didn't hear nothing about the day. Sleeping?'

'I doubt it.' He would learn no more here. 'All right, Royston.'

'Now, don't you put no men into them clubs, Mr Harpur. You let me do the watching. You send your people and everybody is going to know.'

'I've got some good boys.'

'Undercover boys you call them. I know, jeans and tattoos. In the Four Horsemen and Alfredo's they can see the silver buttons on those boys.'

'Maybe.'

'Royston – he the boy for you.'

'It's got to be quick.'

Paine held up a hand to show all was magnificently under control. In the other hand he still held *The Masters*. 'I had a read of this. I got to learn about your culture. Lord Snow and claret wine in the combination rooms after dinner. "To whom are we indebted for this bottle?" You hear much talk like that around here? No good pretending we still back in Jamaica. I need to find out about these details.'

Harpur said, 'A lot of that stuff's dead now, Royston. Another world.'

'Dead?' he shivered. 'Sure, books are dead. You listen to a shelf in the library, it's quiet, not like a dog-fight or a juke box. But books can tell you things. Don't matter they're dead. Me, all I know is I'm alive, so far.'

'Keep out of the basement,' Harpur said as he left.

7

On his private line at the station he made an afternoon call to
Mrs Avery. Her children would be at school, and he knew
Brian was working a day shift. She seemed to sense it would be
Harpur and her voice was guarded but friendly as she
answered, before he had spoken. This was going to be a tricky
conversation, with her husband apparently the purpose of it
yet anything but. How should he move the talk from welfare
discussion of Brian's problems to a suggestion they meet? Did
he want that? Was it a mistake to start this, try to start it? As he
listened and she continued to fret about her husband, Harpur
came to feel malevolent and trapped, the superior making a
pass at one of his people's women because superiors often did.
It was a grubby formula. He chatted on, listened on, and when
his internal phone rang ignored it.

'We ought to meet to talk these things over properly,' he
said. How could he chicken out now?

She did not respond, spoke about the effect of Brian's ten-
sion on the children. Oh, God, what had he bitten off here?

Leo Peters knocked his door and came in apologizing.
'There's something you should hear, sir. It's urgent. I tried to
get you on the phone.'

Harpur cut through Ruth's description of home life and
said, 'Look, can I call you back? Something has come up. Give
me five minutes.' He put the receiver down before she could
reply.

Leo said, 'We had Brian Avery on the line in the Control
Room. He wanted to talk to you. There's some kind of crisis.
Probably he's gone now, but you can hear the tape.'

As they hurried downstairs, Harpur said, 'What crisis?'

'It's not clear. He wouldn't speak, except to you. But he
sounded way over the top, maybe liable to try something he
can't handle.'

Great. A man looks for a lifeline from his boss and it is not there because just at that second the boss is chatting up the man's wife, beginning what he reckons will be the hop and skip to her bed. Nobody would know the two calls coincided, thank God. Yes, thank God – a high-fly cop would think like that, feel entitled to top-class aid. The nausea grew.

On the tape the voice was strained and rushed, but Harpur would have recognized it at once and from the first words felt unnerved, dreading what might come next. *'I've got to speak to Mr Harpur personally. It's crucial. Why have they put me through to you?'* There was the sound of rapid chewing.

Then came the Control Room inspector, *'Where are you, Brian?'*

'I've had a tip from one of my sources.' Excitement, fear, ripe pride bubbled in the words. *'There's something big building up, someone down from London looking us over. I'm making inquiries.'*

'Alone?'

'I'm working on a particular name who's been seen here. My source won't let me disclose at this stage. It's dicey for him. Mr Harpur will understand.'

'Where are you, Brian?'

'You can't reach me for an hour or two. I'll be in contact at four o'clock without fail. Let Mr Harpur know that. Ask him to stand by.'

The inspector must have sensed that in a moment Avery would be gone, and spoke urgently, *'Brian, this is hardly a message at all, mate. Mr Harpur's going to have a lot of questions.'*

'No. He'll get the picture. It must be like this. Confidentiality. Obligations to a tout.'

'Which part of the town are you in? Are you in the town?'

The tape ran silent. 'We traced it,' the inspector told Harpur. 'A box in Ross Square. I wanted the car in the area to take a discreet look around but – '

'To me it seemed possibly a mistake to use radio,' Peters explained. Like Jack Lamb, Leo saw the danger of leaks everywhere and considered the rest of the world one avid ear. 'We could be dealing with an accomplished outfit who have our wavelength. Every other bugger knows it. A call to a car might put a finger on him. My view was maybe it would be better if we drift up there, sir, in an unmarked vehicle. Careful foot-work.'

Harpur agreed, although it was only 3 p.m., an hour before Avery would fall overdue. That quivering excitement in his voice said more than the words, and had gnawed its way into Harpur's mind. He could read Avery. This man had spotted Harpur's doubts about him, and feared he might be thrown off the operation and shamed. So he would hit back and let them all see what talent he had, and flair, and courage. He had re-vealed no details because he meant to do it all alone and reject aid. This would show he could play with the big boys. Jesus, that bumptious talk about his sources and confidentiality and obligations. '*I'm making inquiries.*' Harpur felt bludgeoned by special responsibilities to this frail ox. Guilt was part of it, a big part. He said, 'If there are outside villains scouting, the Col-lator should know.'

'Nothing to date, sir. I've checked,' Leo replied.

'Let's go then.'

'Will you ring back?'

'Where?'

'You told your call, when I interrupted.'

'It's not important.'

They drove, parked, then walked towards the telephone booth, approaching separately, one on each side of the road. 'We take this discreetly,' Harpur said. 'We don't want to pinch any of his glory.'

'He needs it.'

So Leo had doubts about Avery, too. Harpur did not pursue it. Shoppers idled in the sunshine. Things looked good, Harpur thought – nice suits, watertight shoes, spruce pre-cincts for strollers. It was a fair town to have in your care, and he would use all the ways he knew, clean or dirty, to guard it. Peters went to ask shopkeepers if they had seen anything while Harpur looked at the booth, examining the floor, the shelf, the directory, the notices. It was the technique of a treasure-hunt, as if Avery might have left some clever, playful clue here point-ing on to the next stage. Why should he have? Did he even re-alize there had been time to do a trace? Through the glazed

27

panels of this bad-smelling box Harpur could survey the world almost all round, and, if he wanted, could talk to colleagues who had eyes everywhere. And all this surveillance was producing nothing. The town might look healthy but things had begun to happen which he could not fathom. He felt not like someone who saw everything but like an object observed.

Peters beckoned him from a record shop and introduced the manager, a Mr Sumner, small, loud, unfriendly, full of himself. 'Pablo the Pocket was in the shop this morning, sir,' Leo told Harpur. 'Paul Charles James Simpkins – shoplifting, carbreaking, all kinds of small stuff. You probably won't have needed to run across him.'

Sumner said, 'Whenever he's in here I keep my eyes open. I wish you people could control pests like that.'

'And this morning he was with someone?' Harpur asked.

'After he'd been in here a while I realized it wasn't just to thieve. There was a rendezvous.'

'I've described Brian. Mr Sumner thinks the man who met the Pocket could have been him.'

'Well, *he*,' Sumner corrected. 'Yes, he looked police.'

'Smart cheap suit? New cheap shoes?' Harpur asked. 'Envious eyes – sure someone is cornering all the cash, and a pension twenty years on is no substitute? That's us.'

'You said it, not I. He chewed, really worked at it, this fellow. They talked only briefly, standing close, not looking at each other. Terribly corny. The kind of thing they do in spy films.'

'Possibly you heard something,' Harpur suggested.

'Chewing. And music, if that's permitted. A customer was trying a record.'

'But possibly you heard something.' Harpur stuck at it. Even jerks could help.

'A name,' he said. Then an assistant called him away.

'The Pocket does some narking,' Leo said. 'Avery might have been using him.'

Sumner came back, a vigorous, busy walk. 'Well, what I heard was the name Valencia.'

'I like the sound of that. Any more?'

'Just Valencia. Then they separated and the Pocket tried to lift five Monteverdi albums. I told him I was going to call the police and the man he'd been talking to skips forward – yes, a skip – and says Pablo had been looking for a set for him and he was going to pay. Which he did. Cash.'

'For five?'

'One. He said Pablo had been trying to make up his mind which was the best version. As you probably know, the Pocket is the world's number one authority on Monteverdi. Your man's hands were shaking so much he could hardly separate the notes. The chewing – like a race. I hope you never put a firearm in his hands. You have some strange ones in your lot these days.'

'You've been most helpful,' Harpur replied.

'Is this, well, to do with anything?'

'Yes, you could say it's to do with something. A very fair summary, that,' Harpur told him.

He and Peters drove fast towards the docks and a road which had originally been called Valencia Esplanade, marking the sea business once done with Spain. The houses looked over mud-flats to a deep-water channel, and a century ago had been prosperous and handsome, residences of shippers and merchants. Now the big Victorian villas were decaying, like those where Harpur lived, and down here many were boarded up, waiting for the big iron ball. Others had been turned into drab tenements. 'Esplanade' had come to seem farcical, and the title had gone. Today the road and district were always called Valencia, or The Valencia. What small crime did not start from the Ernest Bevin estate began here.

Peters called headquarters to see whether Avery had been in touch at 4 p.m. as promised, and was told, 'No contact.' They parked again and Harpur brought out a torch. Layabout groups melted from corners seeing him. 'You knock doors, Leo. I'll take the empty houses.'

Most of the boarded-up villas had a way in, made by tramps or whores or truants. Harpur crawled through a half-destroyed side door and began a careful tour of the first house, moving as quietly as he could among the debris, the bottles, the shit piles, not sure what he was looking for. Had the Pocket told Avery that someone here on a recce for the bank job had moved into The Valencia? Did this rubbish-dump square with Paine's account of the pricey clothes? So there could be more than one.

Upstairs in the third house he found a middle-aged white wino, male, sleeping the sleep of the near-dead or the would-be-dead, walled in by about a dozen two-litre flasks from Romania. The face looked familiar but from a different kind of setting. Had he been a BBC news producer locally, or a professor of something up the road? Such posts could bore people into lushery. The man's overcoat was foul now, though it had cost a bit once and was hanging neatly on a hook from the picture rail. Tidy habits stuck. What looked like a week-old Chinese take-away in its unopened box protruded from a pocket and contributed one of the milder smells. Harpur put a foot on the thin shoulder and shook him very hard for thirty seconds. 'Seen anyone strange about?' he asked, because policemen put questions. None of them would reach this far-gone sleeper, though, on his rubble bed. 'Use a little wine for thy stomach's sake,' Harpur muttered, after First Timothy. His old man would quote it when brought home paralytic.

He had trouble entering the fourth house. All doors were locked and a heavy wire mesh, not boarding, sealed the windows. He tried the mesh at every point around the house and eventually found a loose corner and eased himself through. At once he heard brief movement, agile and positive, not the stirring of a drunk. He waited, the torch gripped like a cosh. The sound had come from somewhere at the back of the house downstairs. It could be an error to wander here unarmed. He went forward in small paces, with a pause after every two or three, not using the torch. Gun or no, he did not feel too bad. This kind of policing he remembered from his first days. Stinking wreckage was the right habitat for villains. They were losers. Ahead lay a wide passage at the back of the house with doors leading off – and suddenly he heard definite, hurried movement behind one of them. Then the door was wrenched open and a man stepped out and confronted him. 'Police,' Harpur shouted. 'Stay still.'

Leo said, 'It's OK, sir. The Pocket is in here, dead. Strangled. An old dear up the road told me she'd heard something. Signs someone has been living here, possibly more than one.'

'What about Brian?'

'Nothing so far.' They searched with the torch but did not find Avery, nor anything to suggest he had been there.

'Thank God the bugger's white,' Harpur said, standing over the body. 'We can carry him out and not start a riot. They won't think we killed him, or won't care.'

'You a Monteverdi man?' Peters pulled a set of records from under the Pocket. He took an exhibit tag from his pocket and fixed it to the sleeve. 'I'll need to get this place sealed off and guarded.'

Harpur left him fretting about security and from a pay phone rang Jack Lamb, in breach of their normal contact rules but time could be tight. 'We may have a pathfinder team moving into town,' he said.

'It figures.'

'They've killed a nark. They could be looking for other possible leakers. You ought to take care.'

Jack would resent being called a nark, even if he was the best in the business. The sound of the word offended him. 'Don't concern yourself about me, Col. You'd better warn that source of yours, the one I hear tell of. Isn't he black, in the hospital? Nice and handy for him, that, if things turn nasty.'

'Any more news – date, time?'

'Wouldn't I have told you?'

'And afterwards, Jack, when it's over and we've got the sods, can you find some business abroad? Europe would be OK; Australia better. Holly and associates will have friends and family. They'll really be asking then who shopped them, and they'll want to settle up.'

'Leave the country? Come on, Col. I don't like to hear you panicking.'

The accusation hit hard. Avery's disappearance had rocked Harpur, done something to his thinking, something to his morale. The man was on his plate: he had pushed Avery into bravado and probable catastrophe, and in place of nooky calls to Ruth Avery he feared he might soon have to take her the darkest news about her husband.

He sent for more men and cars to help Leo search The Valencia for Avery. 'Work as fast as you can. Be as rough as it takes but find him. Alive. In good shape. And kick his arse for acting big.'

For himself, Harpur drove out to the Ernest Bevin estate. Paine's tip had been that Michael Martin Allen, small-time villain with piffling form going back to King Canute, was squiring the stranger about. So, he could be another route to Avery. Suddenly the approaching bank job had become very secondary. A man had died. Perhaps two had died, one of them a police officer. Lamb and Paine could be at risk. Harpur had to take any lead, even someone as sleazy and backstreet as Michael Martin Allen. Pablo the Pocket might have been a better link, but there was no knowing about that.

The estate where Allen rented a place had been famed for the sensitive care with which planners had respected features of the landscape, and it had won a bag of awards. This community masterpiece had put the town on the map. That was twenty years ago. Some of the high-rise blocks had now been pulled down because of structural faults assisted by ungovernable vandalism. Harpur knew all the streets inside out because the Ernest Bevin provided this town with 40 per cent of its small-time and middling crooks. Allen and his relations by blood and marriage accounted for about 10 per cent on their own, with Dick Darch kin of some sort. Forty per cent Harpur did not regard as too disastrous a figure: estates in other big towns, like Liverpool, London itself, produced worse figures, some without even design awards for their comfort. Over the last four or five years the police had fought to hold the line at 40 per cent, and were winning. The town could stand this – a very weak corner, that was all. He had officers lecturing regularly in the schools up here, telling the youngsters who were not truanting how stupid crime was and especially burglary, riot, arson and rape. This did seem to help in preventing any increase, despite what the parents taught them. For the Ernest Bevin he had a soft spot. There was something so sad and shagged-out about petty crooks.

He knew that whenever police entered the estate, telephone warnings went ahead from outposts on the rim, but Harpur drove a small, ageing, unmarked, radioless vehicle, which he had the pool change frequently for him. There was a chance he could stay undetected. Only a chance – a parked car with a big, wide-awake man in it drew eyes anywhere, and more so on the Ernest Bevin. A lot of families living here had cause to know and remember him. He drew up at some distance from Allen's place, the Ford pointing away from it, climbed into the back and watched from the rear window. Once in a while that worked as cover. People somehow expected a surveillance vehicle to face the target.

After less than ten minutes four people came out of the maisonette and walked towards his car for about twenty yards before turning off. Three of the people Harpur did not recognize – two slaggy women and a young man in his twenties, fitting the sort of description Paine had given: good suit, Smoke gloss. The other was Allen. They occupied the whole pavement, strung out in a line, laughing, waving their arms about, jabbering, full of themselves. High? Pissed? No, he decided it was just excitement. The women were young with good legs and as expensively dressed as the unknown man. None of these three strangers took Harpur's main attention. He stared at Michael Martin Allen. From somewhere this dog-end nobody had found a new, cocky, gleaming style. All of them were twitching and twittering, filling the bum street with the din of optimism and gaiety, but Allen seemed far and away the most pleased with himself, and more than that. This failed pin-head crook had lately picked up a loud self-assurance, something all wrong for what Harpur knew of him, something all wrong for every dead-beat Ernest Bevin villain. Allen glowed with power, like a Mayfair heavy out collecting dues, and the women seemed fascinated by him, this piece of salvage. Allen, and not the unknown man, was starring. Christ, what had happened?

The bounce meant Allen's horse-dung ego had been given a very recent lift. Harpur wondered whether these two men had lately dealt successfully with a threat together, perhaps trapped and killed a mouth which had spoken carelessly and taken too many risks. That sort of dirty triumph could transform the mind of a yob like Allen. For once he would have seen himself hitting back, not running. Had these two killed the Pocket, and maybe Brian Avery as well? Harpur grew convinced that he had been right to come out here.

Leaving the car, he went after them, keeping a good fifty yards back. He saw they were making for a pub, the Lambert Hall, maybe to celebrate whatever it was had helped Allen to find a bit of lead for his pencil. Harpur could not follow inside. Even if Allen did not spot him, other customers would and there might be a stir, enough to draw attention. Breaking off, he walked swiftly back to the maisonette. They would be set for at least an hour. He rang the doorbell, ready with a yarn if anyone answered, but nobody did. Moving to the rear, he was about to try the kitchen door when he saw an old woman seated at the window of a neighbouring flat and watching him. Prize designs or not, these properties crowded each other, with nothing as bourgeois as a hedge anywhere. He knocked on the door instead of trying to bust it, and when there was no reply he walked away, the old woman still staring. But he knew he had to get in and look around. In the streets nearby he searched hopelessly for an unbuggered telephone box to call the station and see whether there was any news of Avery. After about forty minutes he returned to the rear of Allen's maisonette. The nosy old sentry seemed to have gone.

He would have to hurry. When the kitchen door did not yield, he took from his pocket a small bunch of keys able to open anything on the Ernest Bevin. They had been given to him by a Housing Department girl on long loan when she and Harpur were close a few years ago, a sweet and happy kid who had gone on to marry pretty well, thank God. The keys had never failed him. Entering, he closed the door and stood still for a second, taking the feel of the place. Even now he might have been seen. He had to go ahead, though, and could not wait for a warrant, supposing he would have been given one. What evidence could he produce that the body of Brian Avery might be here? Wasn't it all fear, instinct, guesswork? Iles would never wear that. In any case, who bothered with bloody warrants for the Ernest Bevin? The poor sods living up here knew their place. Crooked families realized they would only make long-term big trouble for themselves if they kicked up; decent families liked to keep things sweet with the police and understood that there could be mistakes. Policing was not a science.

He scanned the kitchen and then moved on, making first towards big cupboards and wardrobes and looking all the time for breakages or blood. Every few minutes he stopped to listen, in case anyone approached the maisonette. The old woman at the window had taken a great slice off his margin. He was alert but very calm now. This kind of work he knew, and could do as well as anybody.

In the main bedroom fitted wardrobes took up one wall, the doors all shut. It looked as if Allen and a bird slept here. On the bed lay a brown suit that Oxfam would have giggled at. A green, high-heeled sandal stood among make-up bottles on the rubbishy, flash dressing-table. All the furniture was new and terrible, glistening, glued, created by its grab-all makers for the Ernest Bevin and every other Ernest Bevin in gimcrack Britain. If there was one thing Harpur did not want, it was to finish dead on a tip like this. Christ, how could anyone as low as Allen have a part in the death of a police officer? This scented, gross room proclaimed to Harpur at full pitch that he was in the hole of the enemy and that the enemy had by some trick or dirty luck won a victory. In his grief and anger he could not immediately bring himself to open the wardrobe doors. His interlude of calm had been short. He suffered a vision of what Avery might look like in there, dumped and huddled, eyes still open, gum wad still in his frozen mouth. But visions were something he could do without. Keeping away from the window he stepped across the room and gingerly pulled open the first of the two doors. As he pushed the hanging clothes aside he was sniffing for any of the accompaniment of a violent death: the smell of cordite, or sweat, or urine. At first more suits in Allen's derelict style obscured his view. Then, beneath, he made out two large cardboard boxes. Harpur lifted a flap and saw half a dozen Leica cameras. Allen had always handled opticals. There was nothing else.

Suddenly he became very still, crouched near these boxes, his head inside the wardrobe. From the street he heard the footsteps of several people and male voices, booze-breezy and raw. He quietened his breathing and looked for a possible weapon, but found only the Leicas. Picking up one of them he weighed it in his palm. Wielded like a fist it might do some damage. The front door opened with a bang and the voices grew louder. Now he could make out the slags, too, fluting after rum and black. Quietly, still crouched, he turned, then stood so that he was at least upright facing the bedroom door, which he had left ajar. Anyone turning towards the bedroom would see the open wardrobe through that gap. He should not have come alone and unarmed. Harpur still breathed scent, and it smelled like catastrophe.

Good God, but there had been some bad changes. A year ago, a week ago, if he had been surprised turning over this tinselled nest he would have strolled out of the room now and confronted Allen, and anyone with him, especially when there was a slice of loot like this Leica to shove under his nose. It would have been no more than a ritual, with Allen knowing the part he had to play – villain rumbled. No question of protest or resistance; the police had a right of way through his den. But now Harpur stood and waited, a bit afraid, uncertain whether he would get out, clutching the silly, expensive weapon. How could someone like Allen make him feel the days of easy winning, any winning, had gone? There were times when he saw this town slipping from him.

The voices did not approach, though. Instead, he heard the front door open again and one of the women begin shouting that they should hurry. Allen swore genially at her, but must have obeyed because in a moment the door closed once more. A car started and moved away at speed.

Harpur hardly waited for the sound to recede. Turning to the second wardrobe he pulled the door open. A large number of a woman's dresses and suits hung there. Again it took him a few moments to clear a view of all the floor beneath. There he found a hair-drier and two cups stained with mildewed coffee. Nothing else. So, had it all been panic, imagination, the conviction that Avery's corpse was hidden here? Swiftly he went through the rest of the place discovering nothing of interest but some shop trays of junk jewellery half hidden in a crockery cupboard. Returning to the bedroom he replaced the Leica, then checked through the maisonette to make sure he had left no trace.

He let himself out the back way, relocking the door. The old biddy was in place again, and he gave her what he hoped was a disarming wave. Disarming? It angered him that here, on the Ernest Bevin, where he and every copper had always done what he liked, he should worry about this creased snoop. He changed his mind and turning, he went briskly back to the rear door and let himself in, ignoring the woman at the window. Sod her, sod them all, they did not count.

You showed who was boss. He had to prove he did not pussyfoot. In any case, he had realized as soon as he was outside that he had done only a sketchy search. Because he had been looking for a body and a bit frantic as he worked, he had neglected everything else. Now, he opened drawers left alone before and went through all of Allen's clothes, though still trying to leave no trace.

It was in the palsied brown suit on the bed that he made his find. For someone of Allen's skills the stuff was well hidden. Harpur had seen the trick before, three or four times before, but he was surprised all the same that Allen knew it, and more surprised that he could be bothered to use it. In one pocket was a near-full box of matches. Harpur emptied them into his hand and there on the inside bottom in tiny script was a telephone number. Harpur made a note, and would have bet at that moment that Rex Holly or one of his people could be reached there. Had Allen been taking a correspondence course in security? Harpur replaced the matches and put the box back. It might not be like Allen to take precautions but it was like him to take precautions and then leave the box to be found.

In other pockets of the dun ensemble he found a letter from Helen's Boutique demanding payment for purchase of £245 worth of clothes by someone referred to as Mrs Allen. Where was she? Neither of the two women here today fitted. He found, too, half a dozen betting slips with names on which rang no bells as winners. Yes, Allen was still Allen, and Harpur could wrap this bastard up and wrap up any bastards mad enough to use him.

Barton and Iles wanted to see him when he returned to headquarters. Both were in dress uniform for a Princess of Wales function that evening in the town hall. How did you link these stiff, stately figures with the grubby practice of policing?

'The Pocket's death is on radio and television, and will make the last edition of the press,' Iles groused. 'Pictures of that bloody slum street and the dump interior of the house. It's not something one wants pushed under the fine nose of a beautiful young royal on her first official visit here.'

'Worse things happen within half a mile of Buck House,' Harpur told them.

'That's London,' Barton said, 'the world's unrivalled top shit-heap. This is – was – a clean town. One has fought to make it so.' He shook the long face, full of yearning to be put out to grass.

'The radio is openly referring to the Pocket as "sneak thief and police informer",' Iles intoned. 'It's mucky.'

'Then Avery's disappearance,' Barton said.

'Has that made the media?' Harpur asked.

'Not yet. It will,' Iles said. 'We're instituting a discreet search. We'll try to keep it quiet for as long as possible. I've been in touch with his wife to break the news. We've got someone inside the house with her, and will put a tap on in case there's a contact. She tells me you've been most helpful and friendly.' He gazed at Harpur, perhaps trying to gauge how friendly.

'He's one of my people.'

'Of course,' Iles remarked.

'How does all this add up, Colin?' Barton asked wearily.

'Holly has sent someone ahead to make sure there are no loose ends. Maybe more than one. The Pocket got in the way.'

'And Avery?' Barton asked.

'Possibly.'

'So when are they going to damn well hit us at the bank?' Iles asked.

'It's got to be very imminent – I mean, all these preparations,' Barton said.

'I'm still waiting for the tip,' Harpur told him.

'If your tipster is not hit first. Or tipsters.'

'I've warned them.'

Barton sharpened his fears. 'Tips can go very wrong. It happened on your first outing. Suppose your man gets it too late, not too early, next time?'

'I –'

'We're talking here – it could be going on.' Barton walked to the window, maybe expecting to see the getaway car burning up the street and hear Holly chuckling. 'It's like a damn town under siege. I'm sick of the whole thing, sick to here.' He touched his eyebrows. Why couldn't it be all banquets, ceremonial and order? 'You'll want a replacement for Avery.'

'We'll find Brian, sir.'

'Someone who can shoot like Wyatt Earp, I suppose?'

'That's important.'

'Shoot first, think next.' Barton shrugged, as if today's policing methods were altogether too much. Colourful and gleaming, he walked back to his desk. 'I have to make a speech on the control of crime. Marvellous.'

39

8

Next night Harpur was called urgently to The Valencia. Looking sleepless but bright with triumph, Leo Peters met him at the door of the Incident Room. 'We've found the last person to see the Pocket alive. There could be a lead to Brian,' he said. 'A whore. We can talk to her now. She was in the derelict house with the Pocket just after 2 p.m. Lot of lunchtime trade here.'

'Good work, Leo.'

They drove as if kerb-siding for girls. Then Peters left the car and walked to a couple of tarts in a doorway. He came back with one.

'Nobody's going to believe I'd go with punters in a heap like this,' she said.

'This is Michelle-Anne, sir.'

Harpur nodded. She was about twenty-two, with a South Wales accent and smelling of something quite refined, her clothes pretty. 'Business steady?'

'Better than Coventry, I can tell you. It's all them fucking Nip cars.'

Harpur drove down to the spot where they'd found the Pocket. She was edgy. 'Can't stay away too long. These are the rich hours when the clubs chuck out, midnight till two.'

'Just talk about the Pocket,' Harpur said.

'He been a customer of mine, only once before. He almost never got no money.'

'You go into these dumps in clothes like that?' Harpur asked.

'Not usually. I got a place, nice, books on the shelves. Now listen, I'm helping you and I don't want no trouble there from your people.'

'Don't worry,' Peters told her. 'This is Mr Harpur. He says what goes.'

'I know he's bloody Harpur. I still don't want no trouble.'

'No trouble,' Harpur said.

'It's quick in them old houses. All right in the day – you can see what you're lying on. A couple of five-minute turns pays for a lot of cleaning. Anyway, yesterday it was the Pocket who wanted to go in there. He was in a hell of a hurry, not hot for it, but scared of something. He needed to be off the street. I don't think he was looking for business at all, just wanted to be with someone, anyone he knew, and out of sight. A real gallop into the house. You would of thought he been behind the wall for five years and I'm the first pussy. Something else that's funny: he's carrying records done up in a parcel – I mean, something bought. I never heard of the Pocket buying nothing before.'

'Except pussy,' Peters said.

'Any sign of someone with him?'

'Nothing. I heard you got a man missing, but nobody anywhere who looks like a cop. At first I thought people from the shop must be after him, the way he's shivering. We gets in the house and he's looking through cracks in the boards, watching the street, not saying nothing and not making no play. Well, I asks him if he got money and says I'm not doing it for LPs. And he's got fives, quite a few fives. I thought maybe he'd had his hand in a till. He don't usually do that, but if the chance come, I thought . . . Then the poor love can't get a hard on he's so scared. He's nearly crying and still shaking. It's like being with a kid, his sad little dick all shrunk up with fright and no good to anyone except for laughs. I didn't. When you see someone you know in a mess like that, even someone like the Pocket, you got to worry, haven't you? But I couldn't stay too long, there's other toms to see to. The afternoons – you got to be quick to get what's going. When he seen I was getting ready to leave he really did start crying, and he's trying to get a shine on with one hand and pulling out fives with the other, pushing them at me. Look, Mr Harpur, I wasn't going to charge him. I mean, if it was someone I didn't know and he can't do it, hard shit, I still wants my money – there's my time gone and I got a man to pay. But the Pocket, well, I would only take one of them fives. But he kept shoving the others at me, he wanted me to stay, that's all it was. Just five minutes more company. So he starts talking, trying to show what a big guy he is usually – all these big people he knows and how he can put things right for me with the police because he knows one of Harpur's boys, and he said his name, Brian something. This the boy who's missing?'

'Could be,' Peters replied.

'The Pocket says he can put in a word for me and it would reach the top, and he said everybody was scared of him because he knew a lot – he knew things about a big team who was coming here soon to do a job. There he was, standing with his poor little thing in his hand, talking like King Kong. So you want to know which big boys he was talking about, yes? You think these were the people he was scared of?'

'Could be,' Peters said. Never tell anybody anything.

'I could see it might be a bit important so I'm listening. I mean, I didn't know he was going to get it like that, but I could see anyone who could scare so bad must be big. One name is Holly. Another is Young and one is Gordon. Do you know these names?'

'Two sound right,' Harpur replied. Young might be the pathfinder he'd seen with Michael Martin Allen. 'Did you get the idea he had met any of these men?'

'He said he knew about them, that's all.'

'Did it seem to you any of them were in the town now? Do you think he could have been looking for one of them, or more than one, when he went to the window?' Peters asked.

'How do I know? All I can tell you, he wasn't looking for no friends when he was at them windows. What he said was, he was in danger because some of these big boys from up London had heard about grasses down here and they had sent someone to sort it out. He was scared they knew about him, he was not sure. But they did know about some sooty who talks to police. This one works in the hospital and he meets some cop in the lift and shoots his gob, regular in a lift in the hospital, they had a tip on it. You know this blackie, Mr Harpur?'

'No.'

'This is a nark who gives the police little bits of fuck-all usually, so they don't touch his ganja game. This one is always smelling of sweet dreams and acting the Uncle Tom. Well, he

42

come to know something big by accident or something. That's why they wants him.'

'What about the policeman – Brian? Did the Pocket say where he was? Did you understand they might be seeing each other again soon?' Harpur asked.

'He talked like they was seeing each other all the time, because this Brian thought so much of him.'

'How long did you stay with him?' Peter asked.

'Well, he's in such a state – maybe a quarter of an hour.'

'Did he leave with you?' Peter said.

'He was too afraid. He was scared to be in the street and scared to go home. Somebody knew where he lived, you could see that. Then he says I can have the records, he don't want them. No use to me. It don't look right carrying a parcel, the punters might think you was a shopper, and you'd lose. Last I seen of him, he's at the window again.'

She had become very restless. 'God, it's late. Can you drive me back? My friend will want to know what I've done with the takings. He can be a bastard.' She seemed unlikely to tell them any more. If there had been need of more confirmation, she had provided it: the town had been invaded by Holly's vanguard and they knew much too much. Christ, *everybody* had Royston Paine marked. Harpur drove back.

As they drew up near her beat, Michelle-Anne, or whatever her real name was, hissed, 'Look at that moonlighting cow, stealing my bloody business. They're here all the time, cowboy pussy, housewives. Christ, but I'll have her.'

A woman in her early thirties was slowly walking the pavement, stopping people who came along and talking hard to everybody who would listen. She seemed to show them something held in her hand, maybe a picture. Almost all the encounters were with men, because it was men who prowled in the middle of the night, but to Harpur it looked a strange pick-up technique, and she was getting no takers.

'Let me out,' Michelle-Anne demanded.

'Hang on.' Harpur left the car and went ahead of her to the woman. Her took her arm. 'Mrs Avery, Ruth. This isn't the way to find Brian.'

She did not pull away but turned and faced him. 'Why not? Who says you've got a better one?'

Fair enough. 'These men – they're one-nighters down here. They can't tell you anything about yesterday.'

'The pimps? The girls?' she replied. 'Have you got a better way of searching?' she asked again, gently, as if genuinely looking for an answer, not trying to down him. 'Why are you here, anyway?' Then she did break away from Harpur and approached a bit of court fodder, white in a cream fur coat and wide-brimmed hat, who was spitting abuse at Michelle-Anne. Maybe Harpur should have recognized him.

'Excuse me, sir,' Ruth Avery said to him, 'can you help me? I'm looking for this man.'

He turned and took in Harpur standing near her. Without looking at the photograph he said, 'Never seen him.'

'I'm not police or anything,' she pleaded. 'It's my husband.'

'Never seen him, I told you,' he said, still not looking at the picture. 'Get lost, will you. If he's with a girl he'll come back. You ought to take care of him better, didn't you? He wouldn't want to come down here then.' He switched back to chewing up Michelle-Anne.

Harpur took hold of a big handful of the fur and spun him. 'Now, Brer Rabbit, stop being so snappy. She's been helping us. If I hear any whisper she's had trouble from you or yours, I'll come back and skin you.'

'OK, OK.' He moved away up the street to another girl.

'Keep in touch,' Harpur told Michelle-Anne.

Mrs Avery had also walked on, still flashing the picture. Harpur caught up with her. 'You ought to go back now. I thought we had someone at the house with you?'

'I gave her the slip. I heard a whisper Brian had been down here.'

'Well, leave it now.'

She took a couple more steps away from him, then came back. 'He's not dead, is he? Why would he be killed?'

'No, no. We're going to find him. There's a huge trawl going on.'

'Why should he be killed?' she repeated. 'Did he know too

much? Brian know too much? I can't believe it. He's nothing much as a copper, is he? What would he know?'

It was painful to hear her run him down like that, here, now. 'He's a good man.'

'You do want to find him? You care?' She had leaned forward, spoken intimately, though nobody was near to overhear.

It could be a reference to the pass he had tried. Would he like her husband out of the way? Christ, what was she thinking about? He had been looking for a-change-is-as-good-as-a-monkey-gland thing with her, that was all; not grand, everlasting passion. She must have known that. Again he felt bad and ashamed, shaken that a bit of fooling should be misread. Could stress have put her brain askew? 'We're all working to find him,' he replied. 'And we will.'

'I don't know how a man can disappear in a town this size unless – unless it's bad.'

Neither did Harpur but he said, 'He could be deliberately lying low. He was on to something. We're expecting some big and very rough developments any day.'

Momentarily she bucked up at the idea that Brian might be deep into something crucial, and Harpur was able to lead her back to her car and watch her leave. Nearby, Michelle-Anne was climbing into a new Rover driven by what looked to Harpur like a seventy-year-old dwarf. Her pimp stood back and gazed at his watch.

Harpur drove Peters home, and then went to the hospital and waited in the basement for the freight lift to come down. It was time to tell Paine to get out of town, even if it meant losing one possible source of the raid date. Royston had no cover left: Jack Lamb had picked up his name somewhere, and now a whore on The Valencia could describe him. Would Barton agree to pay something towards a hide-out for the next few weeks? That would strike the Chief as part of the dirty side of policing, something he steered clear of, left to others. Harpur had heard him speak contemptuously of supergrasses. Royston would never rate as one of those, not even as a second-string grass, but Barton was unlikely to distinguish. Paine would have to find his own bolthole.

After an hour the lift came down, but a different porter brought out refuse bags. Harpur kept out of sight and watched until the lift went back up. Towards dawn it descended again and the same man, in an overcoat now, came out and walked away down the underground corridor. Harpur would have to take a risk. He walked quickly after him and asked about Paine. 'Sick or something. Been off two days,' the porter said.

'He's all right?'

'No, he's sick. Who wants to know?'

'From the union.'

'This time of night?'

'When is he coming back?'

'Search me.'

'Are you working here tomorrow – on that lift?'

'Who wants to know?'

Harpur drove up past Paine's house. It was dark and seemed as peaceful as every other house in the street that early. There could be no question of calling. That might really and finally put the finger on Paine, if the finger had not already been put. Harpur went home then and slept.

9

Harpur took another trip to the Ernest Bevin estate and to Michael Martin Allen's maisonette. This sad nobody somehow linked all sides of a frightening, bewildering case. Allen was in touch with the Londoners, he knew the town, probably even knew what the Londoners were trying to do to the town. The Pocket was part of that, so was Avery. Harpur had a duty to lean on Allen, squeeze everything out while there was time . . . if there was time for Avery. None for the Pocket.

An ageing blue van stood outside Allen's front door today, about his derelict mark. After half an hour he appeared carrying what looked like one of the big cardboard boxes full of Leicas that Harpur had found in the wardrobe. The old furtiveness and the old jumpiness were back. This was the Allen he knew, all that wonderful bounce shown with those two birds and the young smart-arse had now vanished. Perhaps the gorgeous friends were gone, too. Allen saw him at once and faltered, then with a pathetic stab at boldness continued as if nothing was wrong and loaded the box into the van. He ignored Harpur and made for the cab.

'How's Allen Enterprises then, Mike?'

'I'm in a hurry now, Mr Harpur. That OK with you?'

'Not really. I'm looking for a little information around the Ernest Bevin. You happen to be on my list.'

'I always bleeding am.'

'That's what it means, Mike, "known to the police". We nurse the connection.' Allen gave up hope of driving away and came and stood with Harpur. 'What's your line these days, Mike?'

'Light haulage.'

'Associates?' Harpur made no move to look in the back.

'Just me, solo. I like it.'

'Associates can be a help.'

'Who? Who you been talking to about me?'

'I heard you had special contacts up the motorway.'

'In the Smoke? Yes, of course. Customers. So?'

'Was one of them visiting yesterday? I happened to be near your place. One called Young?'

'I was with friends yesterday.'

'What friends? Don't I know them all?'

'No, why should you?'

'Where are they now? In the maisonette?'

'No, it was a visit.'

'Who are they?'

'Christ, Mr Harpur, I told you, friends. Can't a man have friends?'

'Any friend of yours I want to know about.'

'These are ordinary nice people, not villains.'

'How the fuck would you know ordinary people?'

'Look, haven't I got a life of my own and – ' He tailed off, knowing the argument a goner. 'You was in my place yesterday, right? I seen a sign. I heard. Somebody was.'

'I had a drift around. Sweet little spot. Where's the wife, then? Behind the wall?'

'She's not like that.'

'What is she like? Where is she?'

'With her mother. But she'll be back. She will be.' He almost shouted the last words.

'Let's go inside now. It's bad for your community rating to be seen talking to me. I look copper.'

Allen led the way. The place seemed empty. Harpur sat down glancing around the gimcrack living-room and nodding towards the purple and gold decor and brilliant boxwood furniture. 'You always liked a bit of style and grace, Mike.' He brought out a picture of Avery. 'Tell me when you last saw this lad.'

Even in his fear the habits of two-timing stood by Allen and he managed to act out bafflement. 'Who is he?'

'Didn't he bring you in for the Gabrielle's Restaurant job, when you left a shoe behind? Another perfect crime.'

'Oh, one of your officers? Mr Avery?'

'How long since you saw him?'

'In court, then.'

'Don't piss me about, Mike. I'd like to be away from this place as soon as I can.'

Allen was in the shagged-out brown suit today. It had looked livelier crumpled on the bed. With this he wore a white, cotton roll neck sweater, the sort of flash mode Kennedy had popularized twenty years before, but it brought Allen no aura. 'What's the bother, Mr Harpur – about Brian Avery?'

'Oh, he could be dead. Someone is deep in shit. I wondered whether you or your friends had seen him in the last day or two.'

'My friends? I told you, they're not involved with police.'

Harpur waited. Then he said, 'The Leicas in the van – you only handling them, or did you do the break-in? Cotter's in The Square, wasn't it? I haven't really looked at the case, but I will now. Mike, the next time you come up you could be sent away from all this elegant stuff and your new friends for a long time. A few cameras – I'd rather not know. But you put me in a spot, don't you, pushing these things under my nose? I've got to make something of it. You understand?'

Allen began to shake. Yes, he understood. 'No, I wasn't part of the break-in. You know that's not my kind of job, a big store. I'm not in that league. You can't fit that on me. Look, someone had problems and wanted to leave things here for a day or two.'

'Cotter's was three weeks ago.'

'Well, a few days. I'll tell you, it was a bleeding nuisance having it here. I knew it could mean trouble.'

'It could. Or maybe not.'

He could think and shake at the same time. 'Yes, I heard Avery was missing.'

'Of course you did.'

'But that's all I know. Nothing about where he is, anything like that. They would never tell me.'

'Who?'

He did not answer.

Harpur stood. 'Easiest thing is you drive me down to the nick in that bloody van. All the evidence at once, that way. You'd better lock up this little palace carefully. I don't know when you'll be back.'

Allen remained seated, ravaged-looking, in a big, mauve ravaged armchair, its synthetic covering patchy and blotched. 'Avery's safe.'

'Where?'

'Honestly, I don't know. But they told me he's all right, and he's going to stay all right.'

'Close?'

'I don't know that.'

'Of course you do, you lying sod. That would be one of the things they wanted you for, to find them a nice little fortress somewhere. How many of them are down here as advance party? The dandy who was with you, and who else?'

Allen did not answer.

'These are people who have already killed once.'

This time the look of puzzlement seemed genuine. 'Killed?'

'Come on, you don't think the Pocket died of exposure, do you?'

'The Pocket? Who said they did that? I heard he was in a fight with some youths, local yobs, that's all.'

'No you didn't.'

'I'll swear on my mother's grave.'

'Sorry to hear she died. The Pocket had been feeding Brian Avery. So if they kill the Pocket, it – '

'No. Nobody's going to do a cop.'

'Where is he?'

'Mr Harpur, I don't know. I'd tell you. I'll swear on my – '

Allen was used to finding himself out of his depth and going down. In his crooked life the sound he made most was a cry for help or pity. Now he feared again that the end was on the way, and he began to come apart. Harpur found it painful to watch, sad, Allen cowering in the foul armchair, not a small man but flabby and blown, short on solidity. He passed a hand over his thick, fair, antique quiff.

'How did they get in touch? Why?'

'They needed some help here. I was recommended.'

'What help?'

'Show them the area.'

'What in the area?'

'Oh, God, Mr Harpur, if I talk – You say they've done Pablo the Pocket.'

'*What* in the area?'

'Well, the hospital. Don't ask me why. They wanted to look at the way to the street through the basement. But they didn't seem to like it.'

'Who's they?'

'Three of them. The man you saw here, called Harry. Two others. I never heard no names. They've been around a week, ten days.'

'And there's a fee for you?'

'That's right.'

'Were you present when they took Avery?'

'No, my God, no. You keep making it sound worse. I know what you're doing, trying to scare me into coughing.'

'You seemed damned pleased yesterday, as if you'd been in on something.'

'I'd been paid.'

'Paid for what? Just giving them a guided tour? That's a nothing job, man. How much would they put your way for that, for God's sake? You looked as if you'd won the Irish Sweep. I got the idea you must be in on it all the way. This is big, big stuff, Mike, not like nicking a bike. This is a murder and abduction of an officer, maybe his death, too. He's got commendations, kids, a mortgage. It's going to sound bloody bad in court.'

'No, honestly, Mr Harpur, I'm a nothing. You said so, often. They're not going to let me in on anything that counts.'

This frail heap in the garish chair was not made for pressure. 'Just tell me this, Mike. They asked you to fix them a little place, did they – somewhere they could operate from? They couldn't stay with you, you're a give-away. So where's your visitor and the rest? Shacked up with the girls somewhere handy – the girls, and Avery?'

Allen cowered into the grim upholstery, trying to decide which side his miserable bit of bread was buttered on. 'If I help – '

'I'll keep it in mind. You've got my word.'

'Yes, your word, but – '

'Best I can offer. I'd say on my mother's grave, too, but I've got to tell you she was a right bitch, Mike, so it wouldn't mean much.'

'I – '

'And it could be all off if you hang about. Avery's life is touch and go.'

Allen got out of the chair and stood gazing from the window, as if afraid someone might be watching or listening. 'William Walton Avenue, on the estate. Number 20.'

Harpur stood. 'Who's there?'

'They moved in. It's an operation, to case the town. These are heavies working for someone big in the Smoke.'

'Who's there?' he asked again. 'How many? The three?'

'Could be.'

'Avery.'

'Could be.'

'For Christ's sake – '

'I don't *know*, Mr Harpur. They don't tell me nothing except what I got to know.'

'Have you been there?'

He shook his head, then laughed. 'Are they going to take me to their place once they're in? I don't know what they might have there. They wouldn't want me to see.'

'Did they ever say how they're spread in the house? Who in which rooms?'

'Oh, God, Mr Harpur. And I wouldn't ask, would I?'

'Someone on watch?'

'Don't know. What would you think?'

Harpur stood. 'Weapons?'

'You got to expect it.'

Yes, you got to. 'You'd better bring the cameras in. I don't like to think of them out on the road in Ernest Bevin.'

'I was taking them to – '

'Peach Matthews? What sort of price will you get from that crook? Keep them here a while. No fence is going to give you a vote of thanks for landing him with items I know about.'

'You want me to keep them here so – '

'I can go on screwing you if needs be. That's it. But you've been doing the decent thing. It might all come out fine, even if you do get pulled into a conspiracy. My bosses are not very understanding people.'

'I'm not in no conspiracy, Mr Harpur. That's a big, rough word. I done a little service, that's all, right on the edge.'

When Harpur left, Allen was still staring from the window. That would be a miserable suit to get shot in. Blood on brown shoddy always looked poor class. Harpur had few ambitions but one of them was to die well-dressed if he ever did get picked off, and for preference in a smart neighbourhood.

He could have called up aid right away; should have, maybe. But, Christ, what was his information? A scared, fourth-division villain had breathed an address. It might be made up, muttered to get shot of Harpur. If Harpur called for help he would have to tell them to bring guns. In five minutes carloads of nervy fire-power would pack William Walton Avenue. After all that had gone wrong with police shootings these past couple of years, the notion unnerved him. If the tip was dud there could be accidents, and the least he should expect was a comic mess. News of it would reach Holly and the Lloyd's job would be called off. Even if the tip was right there could still be accidents, especially an accident to Avery. It was Harpur's job to get Avery back, breathing and unfurrowed. If he won on that and it frightened them off the raid on the bank, too bad. At least he would have saved a cop's life.

He had already seen Barton and Iles jesuiting at full froth and, for God's sake, that was before anything had happened. William Walton Avenue might turn out 100 per cent fiasco – no arrests, a lot of metal flashed, and maybe fired, in the middle of a council estate. There'd be doors axed, old women wetting themselves, furniture bruised, goldfish spilled. What couldn't the *Guardian*'s guardians of small-street freedoms make of that? It was a risk he decided he did not want. His wife might start on again about the job poisoning his compunction. She knew how to hatch a phrase. No, as a first move he would have a look at 20 William Walton Avenue alone. Take things bit by bit.

He drove down the Avenue, located the house, but kept going at a decent pace, like some local in the old banger on his way for the dole. He had a couple of moments to examine the place through his side-window and in the mirror and saw nothing to tell him this semi was a bunker or a jail. You could call it one of Ernest Bevin's better streets, glass in most windows, flowers not scrap or mattresses in the front yards, and Number 20 looking as spruce as any of its neighbours. Downstairs the curtains were open and he had the impression of a room that stretched back to french windows and the garden. There seemed to be nobody in the room, or at least nobody standing. The curtains in the main bedroom were drawn, heavy lined material, and he could not tell whether a light burned behind them.

Turning out of the street he parked at once and walked quickly through a lane to the rear of the house that stood opposite Number 20. He knocked at the kitchen door, smiled big and matily and showed his warrant card to the cheery-looking, attractively dressed, middle-aged woman who answered. Could he watch from the window for a while? 'No fucking pigs allowed in here,' she replied, banging the door. He tried the next house and had better luck with a couple of pensioners. From their downstairs room he kept observation, trying to stay out of sight but sure that any alert pro would soon spot him. So he had to hope they were not alert: they would certainly be pros.

'Whose house?' he asked.

'They comes and goes,' the woman said. 'Strangers. Only there a week.'

'What have you seen lately?'

'Girls. Not top drawer. Girls you'd see in amusements.'

'Amusements?'

'She means pin-ball places.'

'Yes, that sort,' the woman said. 'Shall I dial 999?'

'No. Let's see how it goes.'

'I could do two 9s, ready.'

Thank God for his set of keys. When it grew dusk he borrowed a flashlight from the couple and let himself into Number 20. It seemed obvious that for the moment at any rate the place was empty. No lights had come on, nobody had moved across a window. He did not use the torch yet, but with his nerves and his nose and his ears he felt out the house, just as he had done at Michael Martin Allen's. Iles would not think much of it, this routine illegal entry, so stuff Iles. In any case, for now he had little time to worry about Iles's scruples. Was anyone here? Put your head into someone's little den without permission and they could bite it off, legally.

For a second he risked the torch and went into a vinyl-furnished room, over-neat as if never used. Brownness was the motif here, which some people liked. Seeing nothing, he returned to the hall, putting out the torch, and moved gingerly forward. There would be time for only a swift and general tour of the house, no drawers or cupboards, and nothing to be disturbed. At some stage later it might be necessary to come back and make a formal approach here, and if the place looked as if it had been given a rinse by the SPG, the occupants would be uncooperative.

He began to climb the stairs, more edgy than ever now. He had been taught, and he believed it, that going up a staircase a man was at his most vulnerable, hemmed in by wall and banister, easy meat from above and below. On the small landing he could make out four doors, one ajar leading to bathroom and lavatory, the others all shut. By now he felt almost sure the house was empty and he relaxed marginally.

From somewhere came the sharp smell of disinfectant. At first he assumed it must be the lavatory, though the odour seemed too pervasive, too general for that, as if the whole of the upstairs had been decontaminated lately. Gently he tried the first of the closed doors. It opened on to a bedroom, the kind he would have expected after what he had seen downstairs, everything looking neat and ordered as far as he could tell in the dark, the bed made and turned back at the top like in an hotel. Moving across the landing he opened another door and immediately the smell was overwhelming. This room seemed totally empty, lacking even any sort of covering on the floor boards.

He entered and once more risked the torch briefly, throwing its beams into the corners for fear he had missed something, but no, the room was completely bare. Had it been scrubbed out lately with some potent mixture? He ran his hand over a wall, expecting to find it damp. In fact, the walls and boards were not wet now, but the idea stuck. In a corner furthest from the uncurtained window he crouched down and, with his body shielding the torch, switched on again and looked carefully at the stretch of wall there, searching for stains. Once, a long time ago, he had seen a room where a man had been beaten to death. Nobody had cleaned up there and the walls and floor had been marked with blood and fright-shit. What had happened here, which required this room to be stripped and swabbed? On the painted walls he could see where the texture had been thinned and lined by water and a scrubbing brush. Moving along the wall inch by inch, he went on looking, the inspection kept to the lowest areas so that his light should not shine on the window. There might be people due to return here, though the feeling grew in him that this team had moved on, gone for good.

Then, near the fireplace, in a corner formed by the grate and skirting board where it might have been difficult to wield a scrubbing brush, he found a tiny, thin trace of what could be blood. In this light he was not even sure of the colour, but he was sure enough. To give him time to organize his thinking he put out the flashlight and sat down for a moment on the boards. Had he let his recollections of that earlier death room tint his mind here? Possibly. He could admit it, yet still feel troubled. This room meant something. It put a chill on him, battered his self-control and morale. Avery might have been held here, finished here. Raising his head, Harpur looked towards the window which gave on to a back garden. There were marks in the surrounding plaster and woodwork as if fittings had been removed. Could it have been boarded up, or covered by a grille?

He stood and made for the door. On the landing he noticed what he had missed earlier – that a large bolt had been installed to augment the door's old-fashioned lock. It looked new. He bothered with no other rooms, peered into no more dark corners. Those who would strip and clean a room with such thoroughness were unlikely to leave obvious trails.

When he returned the torch to the oldies he said, 'All quiet over there. Must have been a false alarm.'

'The birds have flown, you mean,' the woman said.

'Give me a ring if you see anything – anything at all.'

In his car he wrote some notes, but notes of what? It was a habit, something to ease his mind and make him think he had matters in hand, definable. He put down a description of the house interior, mentioned the new bolt, the raw odour of hygiene, the possibility of bars or shutters, the possibility of blood. He thought of setting down his notions of what might have happened there to Avery – but how could he reasonably do that? His ideas were the product of panic, had nothing to do with known fact, and constantly changed their shape and direction as new fears entered his head.

10

So what did it mean if this scouting and clean-up team had packed and gone, all their problems removed? Nothing now stood in the way of the raid on Lloyd's once the big money-day arrived there. He needed a whisper very quickly. Speak to me, Jack Lamb. And where the hell was Paine, even Paine? What use was a copper short of voices? Where would Joan of Arc have been without hers?

Lamb, at least, was locatable. Yearly in the banqueting chamber of the Town Hall a Silver Ticket Ball took place, and anyone with money or position or both was pressured to come. Jack qualified on the first count, maybe even on the second: after all, his deals were big and somehow he had no record. Somehow? Part of that somehow was possibly Harpur. One day a jury might have to decide, but not yet: they could still run their tricky partnership. Royston Paine, on the other hand, totally failed to qualify for a Silver Ticket and would not be present. The organizers would see no rôle for seedy blacks in their charity fund-raising, not even seedy blacks sitting on a ganja fortune. Perhaps Paine was out of town and in hiding, anyway. Harpur half hoped so. It would deprive him of a source, but he wanted to think Paine was safe.

Although his wife would go with Harpur to the Silver Ticket Ball, she hated these occasions. Megan approved of charity and worked for it, but snobbery and flagrant wealth she found hard to stomach. She has always been a *Guardian* reader regardless, and could be very rosy on social conscience. All that was in her background. Now and then she would talk of an uncle and aunt who had been Hampstead Fabians. 'Poor love,' he had muttered, the first time he heard this, 'what chance did you ever have?' The differences between them only rarely boiled over, but they had grown more marked as he went higher in the police; and occasionally it became bad enough for him to look elsewhere, though he would probably have looked anyway, and did not pretend to himself that his adulteries had a dialectical base. Sometimes Megan called him Dirtyish Harry. She had little time for Jack Lamb. Paine she might have liked, if they had met, because he was black and scruffy and timid; Lamb lived in a manor house, was white, big, flashy, rich. She got a whiff, not just of corruption but of privileged corruption, and found its company distasteful. That was one of Megan's words. She did not understand, any more than juries understood, how police work had to be done, and she did not want to understand because she believed right and wrong lived far apart and could never meet.

Tonight Lamb had brought his large, loud, woman friend, Fay Corby, waggishly dressed in a bouffant yellow and lime-green robe, plus his mother over from the United States on holiday. As soon as he could, Harpur tried to steer him away from them in the bar. 'Jack I've a feeling this thing is very imminent.'

'And so it is.'

'You have a date now?'

'How many times, Col – if I had a date wouldn't I have told you?'

'How imminent is imminent?'

'Days. The big deposit is in the pipeline.' He turned. 'How lovely you look, Megan. Again. Wonderful you could come.'

'She wouldn't have missed it,' he said quickly.

Megan moved off to chat, and seek purification.

'Here's mother,' Lamb said. As soon as he had introduced her to Harpur he went for more drinks.

Tall, aquiline, regal, Mrs Lamb made occasional short and dynamic gestures. The dress she wore was long, bright, floral, and cut-price. 'Did I hear you were a cop, yes? Brass? You here as a guest, or working? Jack's got friends who are top police? I believe it if you tell me, but how did it happen?'

How, yes. 'Jack's a figure in our community, Mrs Lamb. Everyone knows him.'

'I hear this town hall is built where a castle used to be. Halberds, that sort of thing?'

'Some low parts of one wall are medieval.'

'Gee.' She made no break. 'Well, Jack's big and loud enough, God knows, but I'd like to think he was not in danger. I wish I could believe he'd live to a good age, say forty-seven, forty-eight.'

'He's careful.'

'Too bulky. Such a target. I don't see him often, you know. Every time I do, he looks worse. Bigger and more scared. Louder, but not saying anything people want to hear, ordinary people, that is. You in on his deals?'

'He has a very healthy business.'

'And he spills to you, does he? He was always a voice.'

'Inflation here has been a boon to his kind of trade. People want antiques, china, jewellery. His stock is very valuable.'

Music from the dancing blasted to the bar and he missed something of what she said. 'You've got a face of someone who hears it all and does his own thinking, Mr Harpur. So, you listen to my Jack as long as he sings good, and then one day where is he? Can he see past tomorrow?'

'Everyone admires the way he has established himself in the town.'

'His father was in drugstore supplies, where there are pressures. He always used to say, show me a man's friends, I'll show you a weakness. He never went out with less than five thousand bucks in his pocket to buy off trouble. But, like you said, inflation. Who runs this town?'

'The council's recently gone Labour.'

'No, who runs it? The paymaster.'

'Mrs Lamb, you speak another language.'

Jack reclaimed her for introductions elsewhere. As they departed he leaned across and muttered to Harpur, 'There's something about your friend Avery.'

'Christ, what? This is urgent, Jack.'

'In a moment,' he said, huge, expansive, chortling. 'No, it's not urgent, Colin.'

Megan was dancing and Harpur found himself trapped into conversation now with her partner's wife, a professor at the town's polytechnic, or trapped into listening. A standard left-wing drubbing about police methods began. Thank God the music was loud. He could dwell in pain on the implications of what Lamb had just said, while the prof gabbled on. Now and then a phrase ending with 'y' did get through to him – '*Daily Mail* morality', 'Masonic conspiracy', 'dossier democracy'. He nodded intermittenly to show respect for a big though provincial mind. Sad to think of youngsters not long out of school aerosolled by this miserable adhesive stuff.

After a decent time he walked away and found Lamb again. 'You want to know the hows and whys, Colin?'

'Of?'

'Of Avery's death.'

'I – '

'Don't tell me you still hoped he was alive. How? I mean, a policeman disappears for days. What else? Watch the fore-shore at The Valencia. They weren't tender with him.'

'Damn, how do you know this – know it as fact?' His voice was a mixture of attack and despair.

Jack ignored it, as Harpur might have expected had he been thinking properly. But he was broken by hearing what he had feared for days. You did not ask narks how they knew some-thing, and you certainly did not ask Jack Lamb. He was lean-ing away from Harpur now, being affable and grand to the High Sheriff of the county and his wife. In a while Jack turned back to him.

'I don't know how it was done, Col, either the killing or get-ting the body into the sea. Would they hire a boat? Risky. Things like that are traceable.'

The group had been taking a break and now opened up again. This was no place to hear such foul news. The articulate professor approached, bleating full voice at Jack. 'I did not expect to see you in close conference with the bogies.'

'Oh, Lorna, old Col's not so bad. He's got a sticky job.'

'Police trade on the few hazards, the supposed stress, don't you realize that? And while big softies like you are laying out sympathy for them, they are contracting our rights, abusing our youth.'

'I never heard he abused youths. Himself, yes, but who doesn't, these days of increased leisure and poor TV?'

'This is grown-ups' talk here,' Harpur told her. 'Do you think you could piss off now?'

That did not stop her. As an academic she would be used to rudeness and as a sociologist, or whatever it was, she knew about rough language. She would have stuck at it but Jack took her by the elbow, pointed her towards his mother on the other side of the room and said, 'Please do go and talk to her. She likes meeting all sorts, really, all sorts.' When she had gone he asked Harpur: 'How much did your man Avery know?'

'Not much.'

'About your black friend? About me? Sources?'

'Nothing.'

'Are you sure?'

'Knew nothing from me.'

Jack dwelt on that, then shrugged. His mother had said she saw fear in him. It was not visible to Harpur, but mothers and their chicks had special wavelengths.

'Fay's circulating,' Lamb said. 'She'll be here shortly, and we've got articles a bit special to show you. The deals I spoke of the other day – it's to do with that.'

'What articles?'

'Things of beauty, as you'd expect. But restrain yourself.'

Harpur tried to. It never delighted him to hear of Jack's deals and to become more or less a party to them. Tonight, especially, Harpur would have preferred not to know. Megan would be back soon and he did not want her picking up hints. Somewhere here, too, were Barton and his wife, Silver Ticket people through and through until he stepped down.

'Ah, here's Fay now, and with Megan. Good,' Lamb said. 'Let's have a little expedition, shall we?' The four left the Ball and went to the car park. Fay led them to a twelve-hundredweight van, with the hiring company's name on the side, and unlocking the back invited them to climb into the darkness. Then Lamb helped her up and she closed the door behind them. Harpur smelled vegetables. A match was struck, and Fay lit two camping gas-lamps. Harpur and Megan looked about. The van was empty except that on each of its sides hung a framed painting. Fay moved the lamps so they lit up the bigger picture more clearly. 'What do you say to that, Megan?' Lamb asked.

'My God,' she whispered, 'oh, but this can't be.'

As at the jewellery auction, Harpur's mind had begun to race through lists of missing property, and once more his morale slumped. Fay took them nearer this large picture, an abstract – vivid, alive, beautiful, even in these conditions. Harpur knew little about art, not even what he liked, but he longed to see this work in daylight so that the colours could say all they had to say, the sharp blues, the ochre or orange, the swirls of yellow and black.

'This has to be a Jackson Pollock,' Megan muttered.

'Yes, of course,' Fay replied.

'I didn't even know there were any originals in Britain.'

Again Harpur tried to force his memory of notable thefts into action.

Lamb was saying, 'One has always longed for something of his.'

'About 1942?' Megan asked.

'Yes. I wanted "Shorthand Figure", but no success,' Jack said. 'This comes close, wouldn't you say?'

'More than six feet by seven, you know, Colin,' Fay commented. 'It's much sought after.'

By the FBI?

'Where will you hang it, Jack?' Megan asked.

'Mother hasn't seen it yet. A surprise. She loves beautiful things. I can tell you it cost me a little.'

'And will you keep it?' Megan asked.

'For a while. Fay is in love with it and that's obviously important to me. Then, mother. If one is in a position to offer delight, can one refuse? But later I suppose an offer will come and it will move on. Not titled, as far as I know. That's like some of his stuff.'

'Jack, you can't let it go,' Fay cried.

'Darling, I'm a dealer, not a collector. I have my price. I don't think I'd care to deny that, not with Colin standing here.'

'Christ, haven't we all got a price?' Fay asked. 'I'm twice married, you know.'

Harpur could reasonably have asked where the Pollock came from. It would be a natural, civil question, not an instance of police badgering. Anybody with the slenderest knowledge of pictures, such as himself, would wonder how the work of an American, ardently collected in his own country, could be hanging in the back of a hired van outside a town hall wanting to be a castle in an artistically null English town. He did not ask. A protocol had developed under which Harpur never put such questions to Jack. That was the deal, for ever unspoken, binding, possibly an error, but it was how things worked – or had in the past.

'Could go in my bedroom, I think,' Jack mused. 'It might bring renewed vigour to my fading juices.'

Fay snorted and moved the lamps to illuminate the other painting. This was much smaller, and showed a girl, lovely though a little pinched in the cheeks, standing among foliage and wearing a long, billowing vermilion dress, something like the fluttering style of what Fay had on tonight. It looked as if the artist was more interested in the garment and its colour than in the girl. They waited for Megan to make another guess. 'D. G. Rossetti,' she said. 'Or Burne-Jones.'

'Right first time,' Lamb replied. 'What a clever girl you have, Colin. Do you prize her enough?'

Did she have a clever husband? Harpur wondered what a moderately able prosecuting counsel would make of this, if the day ever came. 'Tell the court, Chief Superintendent, is it true that you were shown a pair of unaccounted-for canvases worth – worth what, £100,000, £200,000 – in a parked van by Mr Lamb and his friend at dead of night?

'Let's go back in, shall we?' he said.

'Do we have to?' Megan asked.

'It's the raffle soon,' Jack replied.

In her considerate way Megan kept the questions until she

and Harpur were on their way home in the car. 'Did they fall off the back of a lorry into the back of a lorry?'

'He's a successful dealer. Now and then he pulls off a really big coup.'

Staring out of the side window away from him she said, 'So brazen, exhibiting them to you, as if he had a hold, an understanding.'

She thought like a jury, or like Iles, or like the word-perfect prof. Why should he expect anything else? Although Megan was bright and they would talk at home often about the job, they never went into how the trickier things really worked. Why should she become a party to it? He genuinely sympathized, but had to carry on all the same. That was how you fashioned a land fit for those with consciences to live in.

'Will you look into it, Col?'

'Not at present.'

'What does that mean?'

It meant all sorts. It meant the scrubbed-out room, and Lamb's certainty that Avery had been killed then dumped in the sea. It meant the continuing failure to get a date for the Lloyd's raid. It meant, could he be sure Lamb would get the tip in time? Christ, they might be there tomorrow, and no ambush in place. And it meant other endless anxieties, too.

'Well, eventually?' she asked.

'Eventually what, love?'

'Look into the pictures.'

'Eventually he will have sold them.'

'For God's sake, what does he have on you? It's damn degrading.'

But not demoting, so far. 'I'm going to drop you off at the house,' he replied. 'I have to check something.'

'Can you check at 2.30 a.m. whether a Jackson Pollock is missing?'

'This is only life and death, not art.'

When he had put her down he drove on to Royston Paine's street. That was one effect of Megan's interrogation, though he could not have explained it to her. Her objections that he showed favour to Lamb had made him worry again about Royston. Had he assumed too easily that Paine had cleared the town? Was he casual about him because Paine was not much use as a nark, was grubby and black? There might still be rough, avenging visitors working even though the William Walton house had been empty, and Paine's name and trail were public.

By car Paine lived only two or three minutes away, though a day's journey socially. Harpur drew in a hundred yards from the house and surveyed the street again. At 2.45 a.m. nothing moved, or nothing he could see. Maybe he should knock on the door. This late there was a chance that the call would be unobserved. But his car's arrival could have roused a few watchers in the dark rooms. Car wrecks, mattresses, fridges, furniture, littered the front gardens. Broken windows had been patched with cardboard or plastic sheets. No painting was ever done in this street, no guttering repaired, no hedges trimmed, no grass cut. One day the middle classes might move in like a Messiah and call the place to salvation like Islington, but not yet.

At about 4 a.m. he decided he would try a gentle tap at Paine's door. By now, any spies should have gone back to bed. Then, just as he was about to leave his car, he thought he saw movement, though no light, in Royston's house – someone small and slight swiftly crossing and recrossing the ground-floor room. Almost certainly not Paine himself. A moment later the front door opened violently and a boy of about thirteen or fourteen came out at a rush and ran away up the street, not even bothering to shut the door behind him. Black and wiry, this could be the figure seen through the window, possibly one of Paine's children. There was a kind of terrible frenzy in the way he ran, as if he had been summoned urgently, or as if escaping something bad. In one hand he carried a new and shiny school satchel which seemed to contain a heavy object. Harpur turned the car and went gently after him, lying well back. But the boy was so obsessed with his mission, or flight, that he appeared able to think of nothing else and never turned to see whether he was being followed.

He led Harpur towards the Pitch, a rough stretch of public playing-fields. Harpur stopped the car and switched off his lights. The boy had slowed to a walk now and seemed to be making for a telephone box at the other side of the fields. As he neared it he became even slower and crouched warily like a soldier in perilous country. Had he been called to a rendezvous here? Because a youth mob met at the Pitch and needed it, this telephone was rarely vandalized. It looked as if someone had rung the boy and told him to come immediately, bringing whatever was in the satchel. Harpur left the car and started to cross the Pitch after him. It had to be Paine who had sent for the boy, Paine in some trouble.

The lad finally reached the unlit telephone booth and opened the door. He glanced in, but obviously saw nothing. It reminded Harpur of his hopeless search for traces of Brian Avery at that box in the town centre. At once, and still in the crouched sidling way, the boy set off towards brick-built changing rooms in the middle of the field. Again Harpur followed. About fifty yards from the building the boy stopped and seemed to unfasten straps on the satchel, though he took nothing out. Then he moved forward once more. Harpur walked faster, closing. Again the boy stopped, now very near the dressing rooms. He put the satchel on the ground and left it there. From inside he took a big, old-looking handgun of some sort, maybe foreign. He stood staring at it for a couple of seconds and then forced himself to walk towards the vandal-proof metal door of the building.

Now, Harpur ran. From where he was the door looked locked, and it ought to have been locked, but when the boy put a hand forward and pulled, it moved. He waited just outside and peered at the blackness, the pistol out in front of him at the full stretch of his arm.

Harpur shouted, though he knew that to the boy he might look like one of the enemies he must be expecting to find here, a big, galloping menace charging at him out of the dark. 'Come back, son,' Harpur bellowed. 'Let me help. I know your dad.' Harpur had lately picked up a pistol himself from the armoury, but who drew on a kid?

The boy heard and turned, swinging the gun so that it pointed at Harpur. They were very close to each other now, less than twenty yards apart. Harpur saw the finger on the trigger of the huge old cannon and fear and confusion in the boy's face. He slowed to a gentle walk. 'I want to help find your father.' The boy backed from him towards the door. Harpur stopped.

'So, where is he? In here?' the boy asked.

'Why do you think so?'

'How did you know to be up here?' The gun was pointed at Harpur's stomach. It looked like something from before the First World War.

'I followed you.'

'You the law? You got my father?'

'I'm looking for him.'

'Why?'

'He's a friend.'

'My father?'

'I heard he could be in trouble.'

'So what do you care?' The voice was calm, though the arm holding the gun shook.

'Did he phone from up here?'

'Who says so?'

Harpur moved, ignoring the gun. He did not walk directly towards the boy but made for the metal doorway. 'We could do with some light.'

'You stay still, you hear.' Now the voice had become shrill.

'Let me look around in here. You wait outside.'

'I said stay.'

Harpur took no notice. It was beyond this kid to shoot, even if the gun would work. Now and then, and not oftener, please God, you had to accept this sort of risk. Bluff, will-power – he half believed in them, and against a child they must have a chance. Harpur entered the building and went forward into the darkness, pushing one foot ahead in the air before each step, feeling the way, afraid of what he might tread on. For the first yard or two there was a little light from the doorway, but

67

deeper in he could see nothing because all windows had been shuttered. Behind, he heard the boy start to follow. 'Mister,' he called in a frightened whisper. 'Mister Pig, wait for me, will you?'

'Where's the gun now? You could stumble. It might go off.'

'You take it.'

'All right. Come towards my voice, very slowly. Point the gun at the ground. At the ground.' Iles wouldn't think much of it if a senior man had his guts blown open by a schoolboy. There was the sound of hesitant, shuffling feet. 'I'm here,' Harpur said, and put out a hand at about head height for the lad. In a moment he touched his face. The boy was startled and gave a small scream. Harpur shifted his hand quickly from face to shoulder and then down his right arm towards the gun. The boy had done as he was told and was holding the pistol straight down at his side. Harpur took it from him and put it in his pocket. Then he gripped the boy's hand.

'Did he grass to you? They killed him?' The child was shaking, perhaps through fear of the darkness, perhaps from dread of what they could find here.

'What's your name?'

'Grenville.'

That's what was meant by adapting to a white community. You gave your kid the name of an English admiral. 'We'll take it easy, Grenville. It could be nothing at all.'

'Why was this door open then?'

True. Still holding the boy's hand, Harpur started moving again, deeper into the building. They were in a long, narrow corridor which turned at right angles and brought them up against an internal door. Harpur found this one would open, too. Grenville gave a small cry. Like Harpur, he must have caught the whiff of ganja above all the usual smells here, socks, feet, liniment, sweat, tobacco. It felt as if they were going into a large square room, probably a changing area. To search it in darkness would be rough, a matter of crossing and recrossing the room, investigating by touch. He found a light switch but nothing happened when he pressed. 'Why make for this place, Grenville? Did your dad mention it when he called?'

'Who said he called?'

'Stop messing me about. I'm trying to help.'

The kid clutched his hand, scared the grip might be broken, but still wanted to give a cop black answers, meaning no answers at all. 'Where else?' Grenville said eventually. 'He wasn't in the field.'

Slowly, Harpur began to cross the room, the boy in tow behind. They met nothing and on the far side reached bench seats around the wall. 'Why don't you wait here?' Harpur said.

'No. No, Mr Pig, don't leave me behind in the dark. I'll come.'

And so they moved along a couple of yards and started traversing the room again, linked together, like a minesweeper doing a pattern in dicey waters. Then, suddenly, Harpur felt as if he was standing in liquid, not much, but thick and sticky. The smell of ganja grew very strong. His foot met something on the ground, something yielding, hefty, lifeless. He paused.

'What's wrong?' Grenville asked.

'Nothing. I lost balance.' He switched direction enough to lead the boy clear of the obstacle and they continued to the other side of the room.

'The floor's wet,' the boy said.

'Pools from the showers.'

'You sure?'

'This is a waste of time. Let's look properly when the staff turn up and there's some light.'

'Better now. There's got to be something wrong.'

'Why?'

He meant the smell of ganja. 'I just had the feeling.'

Harpur took him home. 'Sleep a bit, Grenville.' Then he drove back at once to the Pitch and this time brought his car across the field to the steel door. He parked with headlights on, propped this outer door open, went down the corridor again and jammed the internal door open, too. Because of the right angle in the corridor only a little light reached the big room. It was enough. Royston Paine lay on his back in the middle of the floor, blood congealing around a long neck wound and lying in two pools near him. A set of Harpur's footprints led away from the body, and near the side of the room were smudged and duplicated by the boy's. Maybe Grenville was walking his father's blood through their house now. It had been right to take him away from this.

Gingerly he searched the body and found what might be a key to the dressing-rooms, a wallet stout with paper money, including fifties, a Woolworth's memo pad full of entries unreadable in this light, and a paperback guide to British public schools. Had he been hoping to get Grenville in? Was business that good? No wonder he had not been ecstatic about the twenty for his Darch tip.

Harpur went outside and on the handset reported his find. It was daylight, and waiting in the car he turned the pages of the memo pad with gloved fingers, finding a record of cash deals and debts. In very neat script there were lists of names with an amount of money alongside each, sometimes as much as £250. Not recognizable, prosecutable, names but fancy aliases – Big Man, Paul Robeson, Lobbo, White Man, Whitest Man, Psalmist, Quartz, Hygiene. Judging by the amounts, some must be small-time pushers themselves, not just users.

The cars and vans arrived and he pointed them towards the dressing-rooms. When they had lights going he would join them. It was a place to keep clear of for as long as possible. Then, at about 8.30, when he was back in the big room again, crouched over Paine and trying to think, a constable came to him and said a weeping boy had tried to get through the cordon. Harpur stood up and went out. An ambulance was crossing the field slowly, swaying and bouncing, obviously on its way to nobody it could help.

'Where do murdered people go, Mister?' Grenville asked. His face shone with tears, though he was no longer crying. Harpur sat down near him on the cold soil. The boy had his arms across his chest, holding himself like the autistic child in appeal posters.

'Why did you bring the gun, Grenville? Did he tell you to do that?'

'He had it from a long time. He never used it. Who says it would work, anyway?'

'Not me. I'm not going to make trouble about that.'

'You say. All he told me on the phone was come and help him.'

'Who against?'

'Just to come and help him. How did they do him?'

'It's – '

'A knife? He was scared of knives more than anything. Well, he was scared of everything, but knives the most. Can I go in?'

'Not quite yet. The men have to search the whole place.'

'And take pictures. Is he a mess? Bad cut?'

It seemed a strange question. Cut enough to die. Harpur said nothing.

'That stuff on the floor – what did they do to him?'

'We'll get them.'

The ambulance circled and backed right up to the dressing-rooms doorway. The boy walked a few steps towards the vehicle, then stopped suddenly as if as scared as he had been in the darkness. He started crying again, the noisy, wheezy sobbing of a child. Harpur put an arm around his shoulders.

'He sang to you, didn't he?' Grenville asked.

'He was a very good man.'

'It's because of you.'

Yes. 'I'll get them.'

'Maybe they'll get you.'

'We're ready for them.'

Before Paine was brought out, he turned Grenville and walked him to one of the police cars. He put the boy inside, and stood against the window, blocking the view as there was some brief activity at the rear of the ambulance. The doors closed and it moved off as slowly as it had come. Now and then ambulancemen kicked up about being called to known deads, but this had gone off well.

The Chief Constable's official car approached over the field, passing the ambulance as it left, and Harpur asked an inspector to take Grenville home, then went to meet Barton. He was in uniform for some ceremony with new recruits later today. The outfit suited him, seemed to give his spare, ageing body extra substance. The ribbons looked earned. He appeared svelte, passably resolute.

'We haven't got anyone yet, Colin?'

'Not so far, sir.' They went together into the room where Paine had been found.

'Is this connected with Avery and Pablo the Pocket?'

'It could be.'

'What's the alternative?'

'He was a pusher, sir. Could be someone he's conned, or refused, or someone he's been screwing for payment.'

'Or some hooked kid's old man.' They sat down on a bench. 'Has he put good information your way? Is that part of it, too?'

'Nothing special.'

'This bank job, whenever it's supposed to be?'

'Negligible.'

'But something.'

'Yes, something negligible.'

'The good information comes from elsewhere?'

'Yes.'

'Is elsewhere alive and well and likely to produce?'

'He's fine.'

'Can we keep him like that?'

'Certainly, sir.' It seemed a duty to provide optimism and confidence for this faltering man. Nearby, detectives sifted floor dust.

'We're fighting something pretty big here, aren't we, Colin? They're clearing the site before making the big move. Arrogant, careful sods.'

'It could be that, sir, yes.'

'And they're getting away with it.'

Yes, apocalypse had been artfully and spitefully timetabled to fuck up those pre-retirement months. Harpur left him sitting in his ruptured glory and went to see how the search was progressing. Thank God Barton would have to leave soon, on his way to retail morale-building words to rookies. If they still wanted to be in after hearing the Chief, they must be tip-top, or thick.

72

11

Harpur went home and slept for a few hours. When he awoke he found Ruth Avery downstairs with Megan, waiting to see him. 'You should have called me,' he said.

'No hurry – is there?' Ruth Avery replied. She looked very bad, carefully dressed in a formal yellow suit, blouse and cravat, carefully made-up, but her face slumped to one side, her eyes hopeless. God, no time ago he had wanted to start a diversion with her. Now she had become something he felt for, but in the same way he felt for a subordinate – a responsibility, woman or man, it made no difference. How quickly she had been reduced to a part of his work. All right, before this she was a piece of ass to him, not much more. That was much better, though, wasn't it; better for everyone?

'Ruth heard about the man at the Pitch,' Megan said.

'Paine,' Ruth muttered.

'It's why she came, Colin.'

'That hit me,' she said.

'But why?' Harpur asked.

'Isn't it connected?'

'With Brian?' he asked.

'Of course.'

Could he lie to this woman? 'Why do you say that?' Yes, he could lie to her. 'This man was a drug-pusher. There's some war among the traffickers. Brian wasn't working on drugs.'

She pushed aside his reasoning. 'No, something terrible is happening to this town. It's all out of control. This man dead. The other little grass, Pablo the Pocket. He knew Brian. Aren't they both informants, Pablo and Paine? That's the idea that came to me as soon as I heard about the sooty. Someone is wiping out all the dangers, no messing about – these two, and Brian. Suddenly, I was sure Brian was dead too. All of them small-time, chicken-feed, I know that. But somebody sees them as a nuisance, so get rid. I'd bet Paine was leaking to you.

What is it that they know about, these people? Something big enough to explain so many deaths?'

Four million. Yes, easily big enough. In any case, whose deaths? A couple of out-of-town grasses and an out-of-town no-rank cop. Up the motorway, they wouldn't regard the deaths of the three as worth a sweat.

'I know all the official line on Brian,' Ruth said, '"extensive searching", "continuing hope", "possibly involved in work where he can't break silence". Iles has given me all that crap personally. What's the real picture, Colin? Please, now.'

He had never heard her use his first name before, and saw a look of surprise touch Megan. Maybe Ruth was reflecting that tiny moment of half-intimacy when he had tried chatting her up. It pleased him, warmed him – but he would still lie to her. 'That's about as much as I know, too, Ruth. Iles is passing on to you what I've told him.'

'You pick up all kinds of whispers – things that don't rate as real information but could lead somewhere.'

'And we follow them. So far, though, not a trace.'

She stared at him with those skilfully decorated, lifeless eyes. 'Do you think he's alive?'

'Yes.'

Megan took her arm gently. 'Colin wouldn't say so if he didn't believe it.'

'No?'

'Won't you take my word?' Megan asked. 'I know him very well.' It was spoken tenderly, Megan was always tender, but perhaps something in her wanted to knock Ruth's hint at close-ness with Harpur.

'Haven't any of your other narks given you some idea of what's happened to Brian?'

A long time ago he had realized this girl was too bright by three-quarters for Brian Avery. Without being a part of things she knew perfectly how it all worked. 'Narks? Now and then they come up with something, not oftener than that. On this kind of job they're no help.'

'Brian always says there'd be no detection without them.'

'That's pushing it a bit.' Only a very small bit. 'No, I've had nothing from voices.'

Standing suddenly, Megan invited her to look at the garden. She had seen Harpur was up against it. 'I've been working hard there and when I say I, I mean I.'

In the afternoon, alone, Harpur walked the foreshore searching for a body. When Jack Lamb said something, you'd better believe it. The tide had just begun to go out and if anything were to be found it would be here now. He had to be the one who found it. In a woolly, mawkish fashion he felt he owed Avery that much.

The day was grey and full of drizzle blown in from the sea. Except for a couple of anglers in the distance, he had the foreshore to himself. He thought about going to speak to them, asking whether they had seen or heard any unusual small boat activity off The Valencia lately, but he was reluctant to talk to anyone about Avery, keen to nurse that sadness privately. In any case, if the anglers were local they would lie, not because they needed to, but by habit. Moving as fast as he could on the pebbles, he made his way along the new line of seaweed and flotsam. Several times he saw what could have been a corpse and hurried towards it, but found only sodden clothes, or once a mass of seaweed that had somehow taken on the lines of a spreadeagled man.

And so, when he did come upon Avery, he approached without haste, hoping it was another mistake. He had rounded a point and a strong, nauseating smell reached him, a mixture of oil, seaweed, perhaps sewage. The rain had increased, cutting down vision. He found himself wishing he had left this job to others. As he came nearer he saw that the body lay on its back among tins and seaweed, a tree trunk near the head. Avery had not been in the water long and there was no doubt about identification, though his face had been cut and scarred. Either he had taken a beating or the body had been battered against the rocks and stones of the coast. Avery's legs and arms were tied with rope, but the body had not been weighted. Those who dumped him either did not know about tides or did not care.

Harpur searched the clothes at once, fearing that if he delayed it might be beyond him. There was not much – no money, no warrant card, no papers with a name on, some packets of gum, a receipt for records. He put it all back and then looked around carefully. As far as he could tell in the haze of rain he was alone, the couple of anglers out of sight around the point. He walked quickly away and up to his car. At a pay telephone he dialled 999 and reported the body in a working-class accent that he hoped came near The Valencia's, then rang off. With any luck, now, someone else would have to tell Ruth Avery. Let Iles earn his corn. Harpur could not face talking to those resigned, mascara'd eyes, and could not face explaining why he had been searching the foreshore or why he had withheld Lamb's information. How would he tell her he had nobody to bring in for her husband's death – torture and death, probably? Momentarily he caught the smell of that scrubbed out room again.

Harpur knew nothing except that Lamb had been accurate, must have a fine source, must have more facts than he had given so far. Had the time come when he would have to twist Lamb's arm as if he were just another nobody nark? Could he do it – twist Jack's arm? Would it work? Lamb might come back at him with all sorts. He knew how to look after himself, none better. Wasn't he alive and well and picking up big art, while Paine and the Pocket had died in miserable, *déclassé* settings? Now, though, it was the matter of a policeman's murder. Someone, or more than one, had to pay. Lamb must be made to point the finger. Old acquaintance with him was great and useful, but it could not always hold first place, could it? In his anger and sadness he dialled Lamb now.

'Glad you called, Colin. I've got a date and time.'

12

They waited again near Lloyd's. This time Harpur was jumpier: he had seen three deaths since that earlier failed rendezvous, and the warnings from Lamb and Paine had done damage, too. 'Big boys don't stop to talk,' one of them had said. He wanted the .38 in his hand now, before they showed, if they showed, instead of holster-swaddled against his chest, maybe rusting from fear sweat. Not on. Before they took up position hadn't he done a statutory re-run of the standard thugs-charter briefing which went something like, '*Don't pull your weapon until you're half of half a step from dead*'? Those who touted the rules had to live by the fucking rules. Die by the rules? How would it look on a stone:

> Rest thou now in perfect peace
> Who as per the book did pause
> And duly shout: 'Armed police!'

He had increased coverage today. There were twenty-five men, not twenty, two with an additional car, two at a bus-shelter, both armed, one pedestrianizing near the bank door. He wanted no radio again, but two of the other four cars could watch Harpur and follow. 'Law of averages says my grass is bound to get it right some time,' he muttered.

Chris, the driver, said, 'You pays your money and you takes a chance.'

Although it had been a fight with Barton and Iles, Lloyd's had still been told nothing. They had the voice inside, near the top, and in any case if the raid did not come today it might all have to be set up a third time, and you couldn't have cashiers blabbing around the Dog and Duck. They looked for a Volvo and five faces they would all recognize, either from mug shots or, if Darch was one, from the grubby flesh.

Harpur was expecting an estate car. Four million took some space, even in big denominations. Programmes at the ABC had changed. Now the range of choice was *Uptight*, *A Girl Must Live* and *Knifeman*. It was almost a fortnight further into summer but the roads shone from sharp squalls in the night, and people moved about, joyless, in plastic coats studying the stills. Most of them stuck close to the cinema, thank God, but they would be at risk if shooting started. Things had to look normal until they weren't. That was the trouble with a city-centre ambush; one of the troubles. You had the public to think about. He found himself counting them and counting the children separately time and again. Lead them not into crossfire.

Chris tensed. He was staring into the mirror and his hand moved to the starter, as on that earlier outing. Nobody in the Granada turned but they waited for whatever the driver had seen to come abreast. 'Volvo estate,' he muttered. 'Looks like five. Could be Darchy.' Then silence in the Granada. Although Avery's replacement, Francis Garland, might talk like a know-all, he did not chew. Harpur's guts burned and eddied as they always did when fear took a good hold, but he could keep his bowels tight. Not everyone he had worked with on a gun party could manage that. Whatever went on inside him stayed inside, and nobody knew. Leadership it was called. The Volvo came alongside. None of the five in it even glanced towards the Granada.

'They think they've got it made,' Leo Peters said.

'They're masking up in the back.' Chris turned the engine, but they did not pull out yet. He knew what Harpur wanted. This gang had to be out of the Volvo, unprotected by all that worthy Swedish safety-tested steel, and not able to call it off and bolt. Let them get close to the doors of the bank, maybe even inside. No top turd QC with Civil Liberties membership could then flute away for the defence about these boys being only en route to their gunsmith's for a check-up before the Glorious Twelfth and happening to have on masks as a rehearsal for Mardi Gras. You had to hit the modern British jury between the eyes with the truth or they believed what they'd

78

heard last, and that was not the prosecution. In the Volvo, a pause of maybe ten seconds. Harpur could identify Holly now and Alf Mann. Some step up for Dick Darch! No wonder he had shot off his gob.

'There they go,' Leo said. The stress made him shout a bit. Four were out of the Volvo, boiler suits, eye-masks, wool hats.

'Three 12-bore and a Browning 7.65,' Garland said. 'Darch stays at the wheel.' He sounded a fraction throaty.

Harpur forced himself to leap from the Granada and start belting across the street through the traffic. His legs did not give way. That was something. He saw passers-by on the pavement outside Lloyd's staring at the masked men and cowering back. Who wouldn't? An old man held an open umbrella in front of his body like a shield, gaping at the Volvo in dread. Harpur heard Peters and Garland sprinting behind him, and he saw more of his people closing in fast from other cars now he had given the off.

In its tidy little truss the pistol thudded against his chest. Couldn't he pull it out now? If you were galloping down the mouths of three shotguns and a Browning you had reason to fear for your life, and if you feared for your life the rules said it might be on to pull a gun in self-defence. His mind, his nerves, his skin – God, yes, his skin – told him he might be posing nicely to be picked off. In patches it burned as his flesh forecast hits, felt the shots which had not yet come. The sodding body was fitted with automatic pilot to take a man to cowardice. His neck, shoulders, temple, and upper arms seemed already scorched. Wasn't that enough fear, real fear? But he left the pistol where it was. His men would not. He was relying on that. Oh, what a good boy am I.

Ahead, the four rushed into the bank, too frantic, maybe too cocky, to look behind. He could sort them out by their build: Holly and Bunny Gordon first, then Mann and Morgan. They thought they had a winner here, full surprise, no resistance, no pursuit, a harvest inside, ripe for cutting. Its blue light twitching but siren mute, the Granada slanted across the street, and bugger the traffic. Chris had orders to block off the Volvo and help take Darch. Dicky would be no trouble: not even Holly was going to trust that slob with a gun.

Harpur made for the bank entrance, Peters and Garland still on his tail. More of his boys were converging on the doors and others should be round the back. It would be all right. They could do it. Barton would go out full of honours as the man who beat Rex Holly and cleansed the town of vile metropolitan filth. And then Harpur was up the couple of steps and in, knowing that by now, by now at the very latest, he should have the .38 in his hand, but his will to draw still stymied by all the elegant chatter and debate of the last months, all the media blurb and instant back-bench pieties.

First thing he heard inside was Gordon screaming, 'Didn't I fucking tell you not to move, all of you?' Against the wall a man lay stunned, blood hanging in his grey moustache like soup on a dirty eater and dripping from his chin. 'Anyone else want some?' Gordon yelled. Somehow the battered man had earned a gun butt in the teeth. Gordon had hold of an old woman by the collar of her raincoat. She carried a stick and had a dog on a chain, a yellowing sealyham, blurt-barking now at the scent of crisis or stardom. Gordon kept the barrel of his shotgun lying on her shoulder, the muzzle hard to her neck.

The other three were already behind the counter, charging past the desks towards the open grey steel door of the strong-room, waving the weaponry about, howling at staff to lie down and stay down. A thick-barred grille reached from the counter to the ceiling, but at the far end a polished wooden door for staff and customers visiting the manager hung open, and looked unforced. So, more inside aid? The clerks did as they were told and embraced the carpet. Nobody went for an alarm. Maybe they had been drilled in surrender.

In a glass-walled cubicle near the strong room some sort of supervisor had a telephone in his hand, low at his side, as if he had just picked it up to make a call. He did not continue but banged the receiver back on the set and then slowly lowered himself like a girl having a pee in a field. He stayed squatting like that, not lying, and stared at Holly and the other two through the walls of the glass box, his back against the legs of a desk. Morgan seemed to take a hate to him. It could be because he looked like a boss or because he did not get right down or because the sudden thump of the receiver had scared the gang. Morgan had the Browning and stopped running suddenly, swung the gun around and took single-hand aim at the crouching figure in his frail see-through fortress. And it was fear for the life of this docile exhibit that unfroze Harpur at last and made him grab for the .38 in its holster and start the ritual: 'Stop, all of you. Armed police. Armed police.' If it was worth saying something once, say it twice.

Gordon had seen them even before Harpur's shout and called a warning to the others, but it must have been lost behind the mad barking of the sealyham. Now Holly and the others did hear Harpur, and Morgan changed his aim at once, brought the Browning further around to cover Harpur, Leo Peters, Garland and the back-up. Harpur had his fingers on the butt of the Smith and Wesson, about to draw it, when Morgan fired. All arse-backwards. The training said have the gun in your hand before you shouted. You were announcing yourself as a target otherwise, an invitation – 'Shoot me!'

Bigger than Harpur, with his wide face and bulky, round head Peters was even more of a target, and despite the surrounding din Harpur heard the bullet hit and dig into Leo's flesh and then heard, too, the beginnings of a groan – or not a groan but a small, sad whimpering, like a dog hit by a car, altogether different from any sound Harpur expected to come from a man, and a man the size and hardness of Leo; the kind of sound he could have done without for ever. As Harpur turned to look, Leo was falling, not dead yet and able to lunge and clutch with one hand at Garland's jacket in an effort to stay upright, like a boxer hanging on in a clinch. Garland pulled away violently, letting him drop, and Leo pitched against Harpur's legs, spraying blood from his face over Harpur's trousers and shoes. Garland with his pistol in a two-handed grip had to keep steady and there was no time for the dead or dying. He had it right. As Garland fired twice at Morgan, Harpur freed himself from the weight of Leo's body and turned his pistol towards Bunny Gordon, less than ten yards away, still shielded by the hostage, still waving the short-neck

12-bore.

'Bunny, you daft, lost bugger,' Harpur whispered, because his full voice would not come. He watched the man's eyes, all he could see of his face under the navy wool, wanting to think they showed fear, wanting to think it very badly. For him to hear his name like that had to be a shock. It told this sod, if he was too thick not to know it already, that they were bought and sold. To the left, out of Harpur's vision, there were a couple of heavy sounds, like Morgan falling to the ground and hitting a desk on the way. For the first time now a woman screamed, and a couple more followed. Why so late? Did it trouble them to see a thug like Morgan knocked over?

Behind Harpur there was confused shouting and surging movement. He could not look. Gazing down the nose of that shotgun, Harpur once more felt his flesh burn, his neck, face, shoulders and this time his eyes burned, too. Who wanted a blind whiz-kid? His eyes were on Gordon and the woman, waiting for a moment when he could fire without danger to her, and watching for any tightening of Gordon's finger on the trigger. And if that came? Did Harpur shoot first and never mind the old duck? Suppose he hit her, trying to save his skin? What would bloody Iles and 'Insight' make of that? Where was Barton's knighthood then? The sealyham tugged and swung in arcs on the lead, getting up on back paws now and then in excitement like a circus dog, snapping at the air and the lead, yapping sympathy. The woman was excellent, no weeping, and with a look on her big, over-fed face more of distaste than fear.

'Oh, who are these people? Who, I say? How is this possible?' she called in a heavy, commanding voice.

The daft questions and booming tone distracted Gordon for a second, made him turn and curse her into silence. Harpur could move then. *Thank Christ I don't have to shoot anybody*: the thought framed itself as clearly as that in the moment that he threw himself forward and rocked Gordon with a shoulder charge in the groin, forcing him away from the woman. As Gordon staggered Harpur clung to him, clutching the top of the legs like a rugby tackle, if rugby players carried .38s.

Gordon struggled to keep upright and could have done it, could have kneed and clubbed Harpur off, if there had been no dog. But in a continuing ecstasy of stress, the sealyham had pulled its lead taut behind Gordon's legs and he tangled in it and went down heavily now, on top of the shotgun, Harpur still clinging to him. Harpur heard the slight, brittle sound as Gordon's front teeth hit the fine marble floor on the customers' side of the counter and broke, then a moan and curse.

Harpur rammed the Smith and Wesson against his temple. 'Stay there, pretty boy,' he bellowed, his voice back from leave. 'Keep still. You're finished, the whole crew.' In falling across the lead Gordon had dragged it from the woman's hand, and the dog was held close to his head now, yelping and frothing and snapping, the lead trapped under his body. One of Harpur's boys rushed forward and put an arm around the woman, like a prize.

From where he lay alongside Gordon on the cream marble, Harpur saw a couple of men dragging Alf Mann by the hair towards him. They had pulled Mann's mask off and he was handcuffed behind his back. His face looked as if it had taken punishment and there was a thin trail of blood from his nose as they pulled him across the floor. When they reached Gordon and Harpur they lifted Mann by his hair and feet and dropped him heavily on to Gordon. Someone collected Gordon's shotgun and then braceleted him and Mann together. Nearby, half a dozen men were loading Peters on to a stretcher with exaggerated care. It was a mark of respect, nothing to do with saving him more pain or injury, or with life.

'Holly's got out,' Garland said.

'Christ, how?' Harpur stood up.

'Some cock-up.'

'Through the main door?'

'Seems like it.'

'Jesus, who was briefed to have him?' At once he knew, and realized it could be a mistake to ask. One of the things wrong with briefings was that they did not allow for deaths.

'Well, Leo, sir.' Garland rarely sounded hesitant, but he did now. There were going to be questions about why Leo had been hit, and they would come to Harpur. 'But we'll soon nail Holly.'

'Is he armed?'

Garland was listening to his handset. 'They think he's bolted into the Museum. Yes, armed. The 12-bore.'

'Three hundred yards from here. How the hell did he get so far?'

Garland went back to formula and vagueness. 'Some cock-up. Our people are all around there. He can't get out.'

'He's got out of here.' Harpur felt suddenly that none of the four they had taken really rated, and saving the money did not amount to much, either. All right, one of the four had shot Leo, so it was good to get him. He needed Holly, though; Holly had laid on all this, had laid on all that earlier carnage – the Pocket, Paine, Avery – and had knocked the life out of Ruth Avery, unforgivably turning her from a juicy bird into a piece of grief. Holly had slipped away and could slip away further. There were few better at it. 'Has he hurt anyone?'

'Not that I've heard. He'll be a doddle. He's getting on, won't be keen to lose blood.'

'Thirty-nine.' That might seem ancient to Garland. God, at thirty-six Harpur must strike him as elderly, too, the oldest whiz-kid in town.

Morgan lay where he had dropped, almost at the strongroom door. The bullets had spun his body so that he lay with an arm out ahead of him as if reaching for the loot, and you could have tattooed *Crime Does Not Pay* on his wrist. Nobody bothered with him, though the Browning had been taken away. The bank was a closed episode, a victory. Half a victory, then.

Harpur and Garland left Lloyd's and ran down Archangel Street towards the Museum. A scattering of uniformed men circled the big old building, but it did not look watertight. By now Barton and Iles would know things had been less than clean and perfect. They would hear the hunt was still on, watch the flags moved on the Control Room street map. They might even have been told that the man on the loose was the one they wanted most. 'People at the back?' he asked Garland.

'Sam is organizing it now.'

Yes, cock-up. This sort of thing was not covered in briefings because it shouldn't happen, so no bugger knew what to do. Holly might be out and away. They were at the bottom of the big spread of steps that led up to the Museum. Cars arrived bringing a couple of marksmen from the bank, but Harpur felt no easier. He could smell error on error.

One of the men just come said, 'Leo's not going to make it, sir.'

'Christ, I know that.' Was he being told it was his fault? The man's war-film lingo infuriated him. 'Yes, sorry,' he said.

'I'll take a couple of lads and see to Holly,' Garland suggested.

'I'm coming as well.'

'Good. Sir.' Garland grinned a team grin. Nothing to beat gun camaraderie, a posse bond, if you liked hunting.

On his own handset Harpur spoke to Sam Oxford at the rear. Nobody had tried to come through since they arrived. Which would be when? Harpur did not ask. They had to assume Holly was still in there, and bring him out. 'Keep awake,' he said and at a trot led his little party into the porch of the Museum. They paused for a moment and then entered at a rush, spread out, crouched, all showing handguns. At once Harpur and Garland found a spot behind a big, foul slab of abstract sculpture and Garland muttered, 'Whenever I get close to culture I cock my revolver.' The Museum had been built in the town's prosperous past, a high Edwardian place with an ornate ceiling and long display hall downstairs. It offended Harpur that this recidivist slug should find shelter here, dirtying a building that people of the town felt proud of. Garland pointed with his .38 towards a stone-railed balcony high along one wall and commanding pretty well everything below. The offices would be up there. Metal filing-cabinets had been stacked against the rail, making a wall, perhaps awaiting transfer from one room to another. This was what Garland was indicating – as good a last ditch as could be found by a thirty-nine-year-old in a panic.

'You're boxed, oh wizened one,' Garland yelled. 'You won't be wanting more shooting, Rex, will you? A dozen of us here.

You're the last.'

'Armed police,' Harpur called. There must be a lot of Museum staff about, though he had not seen them. They could testify that things were done nicely.

'It's a balls-up, Rex. You'd better come down,' Garland said. 'Hands on head and slowly down the stairs. Well, I don't have to tell you. You're a pro.' Garland moved out a little from the repulsive lump of stone, no longer properly in cover. He held his pistol in two hands pointing at the cabinets. This boy was on the speeded promotion trail, shining with leadership even when not leader, a Bramshill star like Harpur himself.

Harpur, still crouching, scuttled fast towards the foot of the wide main staircase leading to the balcony. Now he felt only excitement, no intelligent anxiety for his flesh. That boy Garland, his ego and his mouth, was a tonic. The others dashed to follow. At the top of the staircase Harpur paused again and kept low. The eight or nine filing-cabinets were in an L-shape, half a dozen lined alongside the stone balcony rail and a few at the end facing Harpur, jutting out. Anyone in the corner of the L was shielded from below and from attack up the stairs. Did Holly mean to fight it out? If he was taken and went back inside, it would be for ever. Why not invite something quicker and do what damage you could en route?

At the other end of the balcony Harpur saw display cases full of Stone Age weapons and tools, and beyond them a couple of offices, their solid wood doors shut and the rooms possibly empty, or maybe containing frightened people who would not be offering help. Harpur saw no movement nor heard anything from behind the cabinets. Should he call his boys in from the rear? They might be able to find a staircase at the other end, come through those offices and take Holly from the open side of the L. To close from behind like that might be easy and reasonably quick.

Not quick enough. He had grown impatient to end this thing. Holly should never have got out of the bank and Harpur meant to see that put right at once, and put right by him. He had to score. 'Cover me,' he told Garland and the others, beginning to move along the landing.

'I'll come,' Garland replied.

'Stay. Cover me.'

'Sir, it's not a one-man job. We ought to rush him, all of us.'

He could be right. 'Stay,' Harpur said, as if speaking to a dog. Garland would love that. On his stomach, Harpur sneaked forward, revolver out ahead in his right hand, ears strained for the sound of breathing and for the sound of quick, desperate, perilous movement. Holly might be able to watch him through the fine gaps between the cabinets. That could be bad, but he kept going and had started congratulating himself on top-class calm and guts when he suddenly realized he was sweating so much that the knees of his trousers were sticking to the floor and only came free with a little tug at each advance. He kept very close to the rail: it felt safer, though he did not know why. Perhaps the sight of police reinforcements in the hall and marksmen covering the cabinets gave him comfort. That would help only if Holly had to stand and show himself before shooting. Could he pick off Harpur through a gap?

Behind him, Garland yelled again, trying to draw Holly's attention. 'We can wait, Rex. We just sit here and have a drag until you crack. Come out now, there's a doll. Push the gun our way, count ten, and then come after it. You'll be safe. We're not the SAS.'

Glancing down again to the hall for assurance that the marksmen were still ready, Harpur's eyes took in a couple of the Museum staff, half in cover behind a statue of two naked lovers embracing. One face he registered with inexplicably fierce clarity – a girl of about twenty, red-cheeked, fat, her hair sandy and very expensively styled above plain features, was gazing up at the balcony, horrified. Harpur turned to follow the line of her gaze in case Holly had stood up with the 12-bore and was in view, but saw nothing. Maybe she was just frightened by the whole carry-on, the guns, the yelling, the rush of activity. Her fear boosted him. His job was to make things safe for this girl and see to it that she could peacefully enjoy the glamour of her hair-do and the quiet of her job. He winked down at her. Absurd. He could not even be sure she was looking at him, and she was not the kind of girl men winked at.

Harpur stood up, impatient still. Rushing forward he shoulder-charged a couple of the cabinets, hoping to God they would go over, and reckoning to make it impossible for Holly to fire. Garland must have seen the purpose immediately, and a second after Harpur's move he came up at a sprint and threw his weight against another part of the metal wall. The cabinets were empty, had no weight, and toppled at once. They fell flat. Behind was no cowering man to stop them crashing to the floor.

Harpur staggered but kept upright and could see now that one of the office doors behind was not properly shut after all. When he pushed it wide he found three men and a woman at their desk, hands on head, obeying instructions long after the man who gave them had gone. At the far end of the room was another door, a route to the back of the building. Holly would have been through and out while Harpur and his people were still at Lloyd's, stupidly imagining the bank was the beginning and the end of things.

13

Late in the evening Holly was still loose and Barton decided on a tour of the roadblocks with Harpur. They had no driver, the Chief himself taking the wheel. He must have reckoned this would make the visits seem more personal. At each stop he put on a fine show for the officers on duty, relaying determination and a vibrant belief in team work, and for the first time Harpur saw how he must have landed the job. Barton had brilliantly learned the bits and pieces of leadership, as an efficient child might learn the multiplication tables, and could switch on whenever it was needed. At interview he would have seemed magnificently wholesome and gifted. Thundery showers lashed down, but when Barton spoke to the units at the blocks he left the car and stood without a raincoat. 'We'll have him, don't worry. We'll have him if I have to take the town apart.

This bastard tried to poison the place where we live.'

Back in the car he spoke more anxiously. 'My feeling is, he must be through and away. They would have switch cars ready after the bank job. If he could reach one of those – It takes a while to seal a town properly. He'll be back in London.'

It was a fair analysis but Harpur replied, 'He could be holed up, maybe keeping a family prisoner.'

'You mean we could be in for a siege? God, I've got four people dead here already, including two policemen.'

'That's why we've got to have him, sir. He ran the whole thing, orchestrated the deaths.'

'Tipsters' information only.'

'It was right on everything else.'

'Fair enough.' They were at another block. The rain had increased. Barton stepped out of the car. 'All well, lads and lasses? You've got the blow-up pictures of this creature? We'll have him. If I have to take the town apart, I'll have him. This bastard tried to poison the place where we live.'

As they moved off again he said, 'Man in a mask, seen mostly from the rear or during a fracas in the bank – we've got huge ID problems. The men we've picked up are not going to implicate him: they've got skin and families to think of. I'm half inclined to – ' He drew back from framing that thought. Half inclined to forget about Holly, unless he fell into their lap? Not even Barton could put words to that capitulation, however flimsy he had become.

'Darch should sing,' Harpur told him. 'He's just local horse-shit, not big time pro. I'll be working on him tonight. There ought to be a deal. And maybe even one of the others, if we can guarantee protection.'

'Who can?'

'We can say we can. People believe all sorts when they want to.'

'And think of Dicky Darch in the box: is his stuff going to stand up? Holly will be back there now in Peckham buying himself an alibi, and putting his brief on standby.'

'We've got the Volvo, sir. We could have Holly's prints there, or even in the bank.'

'Think so?'

No, he did not think so, but he was ready to say anything that might keep Barton from collapse. Jesus, Holly *had* to answer. How could that be in question? Now, tonight, he must make Barton see this. The whole thing would be lost once he had Iles with him, echoing, endorsing, adding the kind of spineless thoughts he deduced Barton wanted to hear.

It was time to offer some competing butter. 'I like your phrase to the people on duty – that Holly meant to poison the town, sir. We can stop that for keeps.'

'These sods are powerful and damn clever, Colin. And lucky. Yes, lucky. That's the worst of it. How does he get out of a trap like Lloyd's? Tell me how.' For a second his voice grew loud, frail, womanish. 'We've got to be careful.'

After a silence he produced more of his worries, maybe his prime worries. 'Of course, there'll be all kinds of shit flying because of Lloyd's, quite apart from the trial. I've had to get in touch with Leo Peters's mother, a lovely woman, but – look, she's got the idea he was pushed into the bank ahead of everybody, wide open to gunfire.'

'It wasn't like that.'

'Oh, she's very upset and bitter. Confused. I understand. Frankly, she could be a pain in the arse. You stand by your version that you led in?'

'Leo and the others were behind me.'

'But you never fired?'

'No, sir.'

'Were you ready to?'

'I was drawing when Leo was shot.'

'Forgive me, but I'm trying to deal with Home Office niggles – could they say that if you'd been in a position to fire, Morgan would not have dared shoot and neither death would have happened? Do you think you could have drawn earlier?'

'He would have fired anyway.'

'That we don't know. The Homos have been on to me, of course, and so far the one point they make is that it was the man with only a Browning who was killed. What they call "the least formidable".'

90

'He hit Leo.'

Barton nodded hurriedly. 'Of course, exactly what I've said to them. Then they ask, did we take Morgan out of revenge?'

'We didn't know whether he would fire again.' It sounded as if Whitehall was in typical form. They hammered you for not firing soon enough, and then for firing at all. Were police in any other country subject to such snivelling queries? Was it like this in New York or Paris or Rome?

'Would you have shot him yourself had you been ready?' Barton asked.

'Certainly.'

'But in the event it was Garland. Bags of bottle there. Would you say impetuous?' The Lord giveth and the Lord taketh away, blessed be the name of the Lord.

'A warning had been shouted, sir. A man was firing at us, damned efficiently.'

'Nobody disputes the warning. Bank staff will confirm this side of things was exemplary.' Barton might have sensed something of Harpur's rage. 'You must regard all this as a bit absurd, Colin – criticism from both directions, for opposite reasons, it might seem. But it's not quite like that, is it?'

'Isn't it, sir?'

'Well, it's a fine point, but the Homos are saying that the sight of your pistol, had it been drawn in time, could have made all the shooting unnecessary. This is the line of attack the Home Secretary expects in the Commons. A hell of a lot of experts on deterrents there.'

'Any experts on bank jobs, or Brownings? Anyway, can't he clam up – give the old *sub judice* bit?'

'What we're liable to get is the charge that you over-reacted – that is, over-reacted to the warnings about firearms post Waldorf.' He paused and thought. 'Perhaps I should have said under-reacted – under-reacted to the situation at the bank, that is. Jesus, what a tangle.' Barton sighed. Was it fair all this should be shoved the poor, feeble has-been's way?

They drew up at another barrier. 'All well, boys and girls? We'll have this sod, never fear, even if I have to take the town apart.' On cue the resonance of Olivier billowed back.

If Harpur had been required himself to speak at the road-blocks he might have said something different. 'I'll get Holly, even though I have to do it alone.' The obligation was around his neck, the knot strangling him. There was the cock-up over Peters to put right, and the torture and death of Avery to square. There was Paine, and there was the Pocket, and the de-sexing of Ruth Avery through worry and grief – which on the face of it seemed a negligible grudge, yet which angered him the most. His mind went first to the living, though the dead came soon after. Holly had to pay. If Barton was neutralized by fatigue and doubt, he would have to be guided into a corner, left to slumber out his last days, ignored.

In the car again, the Chief said, 'I want nothing heavy with Darch, or with the rest. There's money behind these people. All right, crooked money, but it will buy first-flight counsel just the same. I'd like to see watertight, contemporaneous notes, if possible signed page by page by the accused. And no bodily contact sports.'

'Villians like these don't sign, don't make statements, sir. Darch might be persuaded, not the others.'

'Try – inside the rules. We must avoid cross-examination material that is simply attacks on police probity. The press love reporting that stuff.' By the time it reached court, Barton would be very near departure and very near any farewell hon-ours. Nothing could be allowed to sprag that chance.

When they reached the final roadblock there had still been no sighting of Holly, and Barton drove Harpur back to head-quarters, heater on full and the car sharp with a smell of damp, officer-quality wool as the Chief's suit gently steamed. They parted and Harpur went with Garland to see Bunny Gordon first in a secure interview room. Darch could stew, that might help unravel the bugger. It would not touch any of the others.

'Bunny, old dear, I hope they're looking after you,' Harpur said. The man's lips were swollen and discoloured after the fall and he kept them closed to hide the broken teeth. A patch of blood stained the side of his face, perhaps his own, perhaps from Mann who had been thrown on top of him in the bank. 'Pain from the teeth? We're moving heaven and earth to find a dentist, I understand. You know what it is after hours. They're all out on the town spending their loot.'

'You don't look too good, Bunny.' That was Garland. 'The file gives date of birth 1952. Should it be 42?'

'It's the light in here. He'd look all right after a bath and in a decent suit, wouldn't you, Bunny?'

'Suit? That's not going to be happening for ten years, even with good behaviour,' Garland said.

'We've come to you last, Bunny. It's a formality before charging. The others have coughed all we want, naming names, dates, contacts, the lot. You get honourable mention on all sides.'

'What others?' Two teeth had been snapped off half-way down. Even a couple of words gave him difficulties. He sat at a table, hands manacled in front of him, the table and all chairs in the room screwed to the floor. He still wore the boiler suit used in the raid, and some of the blood had soaked the left shoulder.

'Others?' Harpur said. 'Oh, you know – in the conspiracy to rob.'

'What others?' Small, slight, beaky faced with thick fair hair, he looked more like a door-to-door con man than a bank raider.

'Mann, Darch, Holly,' Harpur replied. 'Can't talk to Morgan. He seems to have fallen heavily and killed himself, poor sod.'

'I got a right to a solicitor.'

'You must be pretty sick of Holly, leading you into a reception committee. That bugger's lost his touch, Bunny,' Harpur said.

'And now the sod is saying you were in charge and ran the whole thing from the first – not just Lloyd's, but the killings in the town before. Mr Harpur and I don't swallow that, but we've got to tell you what he says. And there's no knowing what a jury might believe. Whoever set it all up can look forward to a judge's recommendation of thirty years. Conspiracy to kill two police officers, conspiracy to kill police informants, conspiracy to take a few million – it's largish stuff, and leading it is very large.'

'I got a right to a solicitor.'

'If you want to say it was Holly who put it all together, ordered the killings, lined up the bank, the whole bloody shebang, we'll take a statement now. Francis writes a nice hand. Things could go a lot easier for you then. We know it was Holly. Look, you'd only be confirming, not real grassing at all, Bunny. Christ, what have you got to lose?'

Garland unlocked the cuffs. 'We must fetch soap and water for you and a change of gear.'

'You don't owe a thing to Holly, when he's fucked you up like this and is naming you.'

'I got a right to a phone call to a lawyer. I know his number at home.'

'Of course you do, but it's late,' Garland told him.

'Have they looked after you for food?'

'Can you eat all right?' Garland asked. 'The teeth, I mean. We could get you something mushy – Indian, Chinese? You're very lucky landing with Mr Harpur and me, you know. We don't help things along with a bit of welly. But I ask you to see it from our point of view. We've got a Chief here who's hard.'

'Well, he came to us from West Midlands, so you'll know what we're talking about. Due to retire soon and very keen to go out with a bang. They all are. The knighthood and what have you – it's the way to directorships, isn't it?'

'So he wants Holly, really wants to nail him for everything known to man, and he doesn't much care how it's done.'

'What Francis is saying is that there's pressure on us, Bunny.'

'We can't play this as we would like to, as we would normally. We might have to forget about the usual decencies for a while. Or, if we don't do that ourselves, we could be taken off and a couple of boys let loose on you. You know what I mean? Broken teeth already . . . you've got some damage, and people in the bank will say it couldn't be helped – no brutality, only reasonable force, you with the 12-bore. Now, what I'm saying is, who knows the extent of the injuries you got there, what we could call legitimate injuries? Suppose you get a few more teeth knocked out, and other breakages? Nobody's going to be able to say it wasn't all caused at the bank when you fell. How is a doctor to know the difference? You understand what a police station is like when officers have been killed – not just killed: Brian Avery was badly messed about before he died. The feelings you get in a nick are something special then, like a family bruised by some deep loss.'

Garland suddenly lunged forward and grabbed Bunny by an ear, pulling him to his feet. 'Am I boring you? Do you think I'm laying it on, being like a family? Why look so fucking amused? It's a laugh? Is it a joke we're trying to help you out of a bloody hole?'

The anger was genuine and Harpur waited for it to fade. He felt it all himself, and not just because Gordon had smirked at a phrase. But there had been time to get used to the rage, keep it decent, and in any case he did not knock prisoners about, with or without special warnings from Barton. Although he had learned to walk shadowy ground as a policeman, that did not include beating helpless men in closed rooms. Most of his people knew it and would try nothing like that in his sight. Garland was new and had something to learn yet.

Now, Garland released Bunny. 'Sit down you slug,' he said. 'There are pictures around of Avery when he was found. I've said to you already, you're lucky it's Mr Harpur and I. So far.'

'Holly putting it about under questioning that you organized all that – it's the kind of information that spreads fast. Francis and I might not believe it because we've got the background on Holly and on you, but there are other officers who will hear the rumours and that will be enough, no matter how much Francis and I try to put people right. If you don't say something yourself to correct Holly's version – make it clear *he's* the big bastard all along, fixing things, saying who's to be hit – if you can't do that, I'm not really able to give you guarantees, Bunny. Every outfit has its savages, hasn't it?'

'I'd like to contact my solicitor, please. He's over twenty-one and stays up late. Don't worry about disturbing him.'

'He'll read about it in the press tomorrow or the day after. I expect he'll be in touch,' Harpur said. 'As long as you've got

95

money.'

'Enough.'

'Ah, but you could have been nearly a million better off if Holly hadn't made a botch,' Harpur pointed out.

'Listen, Bunny, we don't do that hard and soft rubbish in the questioning. We know someone like you has seen it all before and is not going to be fooled. We both want to help you. Obviously, you've got to take what's coming in court, but we're trying to stop a sod like Holly shifting all the real weight on to you.'

Gordon seemed to ponder the offers, then said, 'Who is this guy, Holly, anyway – somebody I'm supposed to know? Can you help me on this?'

'You piss on an offer of friendship, Bunny. Sad,' Garland told him. He manacled Gordon's hands again, behind him this time, and around a chair strut. 'We'll be back, or someone will be. Keep awake. Try and do yourself a bit of good for once. Don't carry the can. If it was in our say-so, you'd have food straight away, you know that; but things being the way they are I'm not sure we can fix it.'

'Could be very tricky,' Harpur said.

On the way to work on Darch they looked into the Control Room. Maps showed the roadblocks still in place, so Holly had not been taken. Yes, as the Chief had diagnosed, Holly would be through and on his way home by now. Harpur could feel the defeat in the air. There was no excited group around the map and all the urgency had gone. He felt like saying something to cheer them up, but then realized he would sound like Barton, knew they would spot the falseness at once and resent it. 'Holly could be a long job,' he said. 'I'm going to get him, though.'

'Somebody has to,' a woman sergeant answered.

'No, not someone. I have to.' That much rhetoric he could risk without becoming farcical.

In the corridor as they approached the second interview room Garland said, 'Gordon's not going to break.'

'Of course not. Nor Mann. They've been through an apprenticeship. They know there's nothing like keeping quiet. Darch might sing a bit, but we're not going to convict anyone

96

on his word alone.'

'And Holly will make bloody sure he doesn't come on to our ground again. So how are we going to – ?'

'Well, I'll have to go on to his ground.'

'Dicey, sir.'

'Every way you look at it it's dicey. But I've got some mistakes to wipe out and a couple of Pilates to make up for.'

The guard on Darch let them in. 'Dicky,' Harpur said, with grand amiability, 'lovely to see you. It's been a while.'

'What about food?' Garland asked. 'Have they looked after you? People can get forgotten. We could send out to the late take-away. Chinese or Indian?'

Like Gordon he was seated at a table. He had been sleeping, head pillowed on his arms. Heavy and broad, big-nosed, craggy, lined, he had a bouncer's face and body, but a bouncer a bit too old and getting nervy and now, still only half awake, he looked scared and confused, almost pitiful.

'Francis Garland has joined the outfit recently.'

'But I've heard of you already, Dick. Some operator. Mr Wheels, I hear.'

'I like motoring, yes.' He was staring at Garland, probably trying to work out whether this was the one who did the roughing up.

'We've come to see you last, Dick,' Harpur said. 'It's a formality, really. All the others have coughed. What else, when they're taken on the job? Some glowing mentions of you. We're only here to confirm a couple of things. I know you won't give any bother – you'll be wanting to eat and get your head down like the others. We'll try not to keep you up too long.'

'They've talked? Now, is this straight, Mr Harpur? I seen some fancy work by police in my time, you know. Why you keeping us all separate?'

'Sometimes talking makes sense,' Harpur replied. 'Even hard buggers like these can see that.'

'Even Holly himself,' Garland added.

'I thought you missed him. I could of swore you – '

'We missed him and then we had him,' Garland said.

97

'I thought he could be right away.'

'He was never really out of the trap, Dick,' Harpur told him.

'When we've got the kind of info we had on this one we don't slip up. He's tried to land you in it really deep,' Garland said.

'Deep? I was the driver, that's all. You saw that. I never went in. No armament, your men can tell you that. You're not doing a plant, are you, Mr Harpur? I always heard you was straight up, well, not too far off. Holly never said nothing about me, did he?' He smiled, as if they were all sharing a big leg-pull.

'About before. Not in the bank,' Harpur said gravely.

'Before it? I don't know what you mean.'

'Things in the town.'

'Like?'

'The Pocket,' Harpur said.

Darch needed a while to take it in and then again tried to smile, as a sign he knew they were playing games. 'The Pocket – kill the Pocket? Christ, come on, Mr Harpur, this is just shit, you know that.'

'Not alone. Involved. That could be enough for us,' Garland told him.

'You're telling me Rex Holly said this?' Darch asked.

'You knew the Pocket,' Harpur said.

'Every bugger in the town knows the Pocket,' Darch answered.

'And knew he told tales,' Harpur went on.

'Did he tell some about you, Dick? Did you have a score to settle there?'

'I'll have to make an inquiry or two and see whether any information about you came our way through him,' Harpur said.

Darch had begun to look more afraid, as if suddenly coming to believe they meant what they said.

'Or maybe you were scared he knew about a future job?' Harpur continued. 'Say, Lloyd's? This was going to be the big one for you, wasn't it? You didn't want some talky-talky dimwit to fuck things up.'

'That's how Holly sees it. He's proud of you, for trying to bung up leaks. It didn't work, but he gives you A for effort.'

'We made it clear we didn't believe him,' Harpur said. 'I told him I knew Dick Darch and that wasn't his kind of villainy at all. Nothing worse than GBH for Dick Darch, I said, and we didn't even keep him in cuffs. But Holly went on about the Pocket, insisting you had a big part in that. He says he didn't know it was happening, and when he found out he was surprised you could handle it.'

'Well, like we were,' Garland told him.

'People do move on to bigger things, I've watched it happen,' Harpur said.

'For God's sake, Mr Harpur, I haven't seen the Pocket for six months, it could be longer.'

'You won't see him again, that's for sure,' Garland said.

'There's no evidence, you can't have no evidence. All this is on the word of this one bastard, Holly. That's right, isn't it?'

'Dick, we're looking into a whole string of killings,' Harpur replied. 'You must know about it – including a police officer who worked a lot with the Pocket?'

'And Royston Paine,' Garland said. 'The sooty nark. What we've got to consider is, someone who could do one nark could do another, and even do an officer the nark was singing to.'

'We want to clear the books, Dick.'

Harpur watched him breaking up, saw him come to believe slowly that the big boys whose company he had strayed into were electing a fall-guy, and he was it by a landslide. They wouldn't give a fish's tit about him, a hired hand, a nothing who could drive and carry cans. These cops – they were probably telling the truth when they said they did not believe he could manage one killing, let alone three. But he knew there were deals done. London sods like Holly, they were powerful even when they had been caught and locked up. They had money and tough lawyers, and things could be worked out with the police. The weaker you were the harder they hit you. They did not care who they got as long as it wrapped things up, what they called cleared the books. If they could close a case and pick up a drink or two on the way, they would be happy.

'You were part of a team, that's what he says – a group setting things up for the bank caper – and this team on their own initiative started knocking people off because they were considered dangerous,' Garland said. 'And he tells us you were the biggest part, the leader, because you had all the in knowledge, living in the town.'

'You mean you've got all this in a statement that he signed?' Darch had worn a set of carpenter's overalls for the raid, navy-blue with braces, almost a fashion garment. With it he had on an old brown roll-top sweater and in the car he had pulled the collar up to cover the lower part of his face. Now, hot with anxiety, he tugged at the collar to ventilate his body.

'Informal statement so far,' Harpur replied. 'The proper thing is being taken now, as a matter of fact. It will be typed up later.'

'I better see that.'

'Of course,' Garland replied.

'But the thing about a statement like that, Dick – the more it's spread, the more people find out what's being said about things like the death of Brian Avery and torture,' Harpur pointed out. 'Messengers, they can talk, you know. There'll already be typists involved. People like that are not security-trained. I don't suppose we have to tell you what a nick is like when one of our people has been killed. It might be someone they hated the guts of, but a death changes all that, it's like a loss in the family. Men can become a bit unpredictable, even officers who are normally very controlled and mild.'

'So perhaps it would be best not to push too hard to see the statement, Dick, although we'll certainly get it sent over if you like.'

'The really important thing is to put your version on record as soon as you can,' Harpur said. 'If you're going to deny involvement in the deaths and say it was really Holly who organized that side of things, possibly even took part – if that's your line you'd better say so now, Dick, so Holly's statement doesn't circulate unchallenged, not even for a couple of hours. Once a rumour gets going in these kinds of circumstances it's nearly impossible to stop it, no matter how hard Francis and I might try. And we would try because we're on your side in this. I'll be frank with you, Dick, because you've always played

100

square with us, as I remember – oh, a bit of villainy, yes, of course, but we could understand each other, and I always appreciated that. So I can tell you, the man we want is Holly. We listen to the bastard and we have to write down what he says, but we're not idiots, we know what he's doing, dropping the whole load on to you because he thinks you're a nobody from the sticks and haven't got anyone to look after your interests.'

From somewhere Darch produced another smile, and then actually chuckled. 'No, you haven't got him, have you? I bet you don't even know for sure he was at Lloyd's. He wouldn't let his mouth go to you. Someone with big form wouldn't do that. This is just some of your old bullshit, Mr Harpur, I can smell it.'

Harpur shrugged. 'I understand how you feel, Dick. You believe in these people – well, you've got to, haven't you, even if they have let you down? Shall I give you a bit of the detail, stuff we couldn't know except from Rex Holly? He says you worked with a man called Michael Martin Allen in the killings, especially over Brian Avery. There was you, Allen, and three down from London on a recce – the five of you handled it. One of the London team was called Harry, I forget the surname. No, it's Young. It will be in the statement. Bit of a dandy.'

And Darch's smile fell poleaxed and the chuckle was carried away stiff under a blanket.

'Allen's related to you by marriage, yes?' Harpur asked.

'I don't work with him. I never worked with him,' Darch muttered. 'Mr Harpur, you know that.' But he spoke as if not sure he would be believed.

'What is he, a brother-in-law?'

'No, not as close as that, not really related at all. It's through his stepfather's cousin or something like that. Don't mean a thing.'

'Why would Holly give us his name?' Garland asked.

'How would he even know about him, some small-town horse-dropping, if Allen wasn't in on it with you?'

After half a minute, maybe more, Darch said, 'Well, he is in on it, yes.'

'So it's all true?' Harpur asked.

101

'He worked for Holly. That part is true. He was their contact man down here, not me. I'm the Wheels, only the Wheels.' He spoke as if that made him an artist and having dealings with Allen and his sort would be a come-down. 'Holly sent them three down to see Allen, and there was orders they was to get the way clear for Lloyd's.'

'What does it mean, get the way clear?' Garland asked.

'Shift people who might be trouble out of the way.'

'The Pocket?' Garland said.

'Anyone.'

'How do you know this?' Garland asked.

'Holly told me himself, didn't he?'

'So you talked to him direct, before the raid?' Harpur said.

'I don't take on a job unless I sees who's the governor. Look, I didn't want to do it. There was all sorts of gab about – too many leaks.'

'You were right,' Garland laughed.

'Yeah, well, too late now, but Holly talked me into it, and he can use frighteners. If he asks you to do something, it gets hard to say no.'

'If you were terrorized, that might be extenuation,' Harpur told him.

Darch was having big trouble breathing and keeping still in his chair. 'Terrorize, you got the word. If I gives you a statement now, there's going to come a day when I got to stand up in the box and tell a judge and jury. It will be all over the papers. Anyone who does that to Holly – well, you know what I'm talking about, don't you? All right, he'll be inside, but what do that matter? He got people to settle his accounts. I got three kids around and a mother. He knows it. He talked about them in a very nice way when we met, very nice, but he was letting me know he had them in mind, that's all. And what happens to yours truly in the slammer? Someone could get to me. Holly could put cash their way to do that – look after their family, or something. These boys, they got life organized, inside, outside, and don't tell me the police or the screws could make me safe. I heard of too many accidents.'

'Things can be arranged.'

Darch held his nose.

'We can't stop you going down, but we'll fix it so you don't see maximum security,' Garland said. 'We can keep an eye on your kids. How many women involved? And your old mum.'

'Open prison? No locks? Someone just strolls in and cuts my throat while I'm learning how to crochet one afternoon?'

Garland took out a notebook. 'You've got a choice, haven't you, Dick? Talk, and put yourself right with us and the boys here; or try to put yourself right with a guy who couldn't care less about dropping you in it. You'd better make up your mind. Mr Harpur and I need some kip and a meal. You're pissing us about, Darchy.'

14

With Barton and Iles, Harpur had to go to three funerals in a week, and by the end he came to feel a touch of farce among the mourning. Inquest delays meant the third was Royston Paine's, and they attended because they were trapped. There had been huge local media publicity for the cremations of Leo Peters and Brian Avery, big photographs and television newsreels showing the Chief and his Deputy in these two cortèges, uniformed, medalled, tense with sympathy. Immediately after Leo's service Barton said, 'My God, we'll have to go to the sooty's. We're dealing with three murder victims here. Imperative we be seen to treat all equally.'

Was he thinking of entering left-of-centre politics when he retired, like that Chief from the South-west? Or maybe the race relations network had a job for him.

'I think that would be an admirable gesture, sir,' Iles remarked. 'Could you be in touch with the family, Colin? Let them know there will be an official presence. It will bring comfort.'

'All three of us will go,' Barton pronounced.

'If I'm there, sir, it will be like putting up a poster to say he was a nark.'

'No, we go to mourn a man killed by criminal violence, as simple as that,' the Chief replied. 'It could be anybody, anybody at all.'

'We didn't attend the Pocket's, sir,' Harpur argued.

'This man is black. It's an opportunity, as well as a responsibility. Get hold of our PR people and tell them to make sure the bloody media know we'll be along. We don't want to turn up to a do like that without some mileage.'

The beginning of the do was at Paine's house, where the body had lain since being released by the coroner. They were not the only whites present, but close to it. They were not the only men without form present, but close. They were not the only men present who did not reek of ganja, but close. Harpur saw faces he knew and which knew him, men who looked away at once if his eyes met theirs in the small, crowded couple of rooms.

Royston occupied a no-expense-spared closed coffin in the parlour, with a New Testament on top and a parchment scroll of some kind, a testimonial or membership document, maybe recognition of a pushing record. The boy that Harpur had followed to the changing-rooms on the Pitch that day stood in a navy school blazer and black tie near the coffin and seemed unwilling to move from it. He too avoided looking at Harpur. Because of the medals, Barton and Iles made small metallic noises as they circulated, being gracious where they found takers. Barton was marvellous at it, gentle, warm, imperturbable, brilliantly interested in almost anything that was said to him, unprovoked by abuse. Iles, tailing him, seemed by comparison hopelessly stiff but must be learning all the time, and once in a while made a gesture or uttered a word that seemed nearly right.

Harpur forced himself to speak to the boy. 'You can see your dad had lots of friends, Grenville. Everyone liked him.'

'That why he's in a box?'

'Done by strangers, people from outside the town.'

'Why did they hate him?'

'The kind of people they are. Full of hate.'

104

'For pigs, yes. Why for my dad? Because he talked to you, Mr Pig. That's why they killed him the way they did, isn't it? If your throat's cut, you don't talk.'

Through the shifting crowd of unreadable black faces Harpur watched Barton speaking to a middle-aged, stooped black woman who looked as if she had been weeping not long ago, but now had reached some sort of control or remoteness. Maybe one of these kindly medicine men had been able to help her with a special prescription. Even by his standards, the deference shown her by Barton was outstanding, and Harpur guessed this must be Royston Paine's widow. Almost always it was a shock to see the wives of men one had known a while and thought of as virtual youngsters. Their women gave the game away, even if they did survive. In this situation, Iles was obviously lost and stayed at the edge, making no attempt to join the conversation. Harpur edged away from the boy at the coffin and drew nearer to the Chief and Mrs Paine. He found they were discussing gardens.

'Magnolia, cherry trees, wallflowers – we always preferred the spring to summer,' she said. 'It's what I like about this country.'

'Agree wholeheartedly,' Barton replied. 'And clematis – eh, clematis on a real stone wall. Tulips, apple blossom.'

'To make a living here, that's something else, but looking at the flowers in the park, who can stop you?'

'Some don't notice them, Mrs Paine.'

'Some are dead.'

A young fierce-looking black evangelical minister in Pickwick glasses and a superb dark suit began to preach from a text in Revelation about the book of life and the judgement. After a prayer they sang, '*When the roll is called up yonder, I'll be there.*' As for Royston, that had to be problematical. Mrs Paine remained silent, her eyes dispassionately on the preacher, her mind away by itself somewhere, maybe among the flowers in the park or those on the hearse, ready outside. Harpur enjoyed the service, fervent and high-pitched, but not too loud; the preacher knew Royston, but not very well, so could talk about him with affection.

The procession to the cemetery included a jazz band, like films Harpur had seen of New Orleans long ago. The three of them, Barton, Iles and himself, walked in line not far behind the body and immediate family. During a pause between blues numbers Barton said, 'What you and Garland got out of Darch is first class, Colin. It tells us everything we knew about Holly – confirms he was involved from start to finish, responsible for each death. In a way, it's very satisfactory, doesn't close the file of course, but puts it into suspension. As evidence, though – uncorroborated – it can take us nowhere.'

'Satisfactory, like knowing someone in the Libyan Embassy did the WPC but not who or how to get him,' Harpur replied.

'The other two will never cough, of course,' Iles said.

'Nothing against you for that, Colin.'

'Certainly not,' Iles added. 'Here's the BBC, sir.' A cameraman was standing on the pavement. Barton and Iles grew silent, trudged grimly forward, heads up to be recognized.

Then Barton continued, 'It's an all-time shit predicament, Col, but I see no way of hooking Holly. We're going to have to make do with what we've got. Mrs Avery will be upset, naturally. I'll talk to her myself. But these people here today, they're not going to kick up, are they? They understand things very well, despite appearances.'

'One crook killed by others,' Iles said. 'If they can't take a joke they shouldn't have joined.' The band went into another blues.

Barton's car had been brought to the graveyard, and once Royston hit bottom he and Iles did not hang about but strode away like generals after an inspection. The boy and his mother stood for a time near the bright mound of mud, and Harpur waited a little way off to make sure she could cope. As any screenplay would have said they should, the band left playing *When The Saints*.

'He lived in the slime and yet was not without wholesomeness.' The minister had also waited, ready to give Mrs Paine and her son a lift back in his big, shiny, cut-price Ambassador, and now came to stand near Harpur. 'One could say Royston was an innocent, despite everything,' he went on in his aggressive, Knightsbridge accent. 'And madly bookish. He probably thought topless meant the tower of Ilium.'

'I was fond of him.'

'Will you nail someone for this? All right, "*Vengeance is mine saith the Lord*", I know – but what we have here is a fairly miniature dealer with his throat cut from ear to ear in some crappy changing-rooms. This guy deserves your most educated efforts.'

'We have arrested some people.'

'Not the people – person – behind this.'

'We'll get him, for the boy's sake as much as anything,' Harpur said.

'I'm going to have to pay attention to that boy, or he could end up another Royston. I'll work to stop that. What's bred in the bone will come out in the wash. I heard the man you wanted – big Rex – just walked away from Lloyd's. Just strolled out. Do I catch a whiff of something?'

'I don't think so.' Harpur felt a surge of anger at the accusation, but you couldn't hit a priest in a graveyard.

'He's not buying safety?'

'No, we messed it up, that's all.'

'In that case it can be put right?'

'Certainly.' Another imperative. Holly had to be caught so Harpur could prove he was not on the take.

The minister handed Harpur a card. It read *Rev. Bart Anstruther, Church of the Free Gospel*. On the back was a text, *Without shedding of blood is no remission*. Presently he said, 'You're going to see to it – you personally?'

'I think so.' What options existed?

Mrs Paine was tugging the boy away from the hole.

Anstruther said, 'Well, I believe you, Mr Harpur, until it gets so I can't.'

15

That farewell from the minister dug a deeper mark into
Harpur's mind than the threatening text from Revelation. He
had been guilty of big, big talk and the preacher had not
needed his half-moon specs to spot it. Bring in Holly personally? How? What had pushed him into such stupid loud-
mouthing? He must have been knocked off balance by the little
black man and by the clever insolence of Paine's mourning
son. If Barton said there could be no hunt for Holly, there
would be no hunt. Harpur was not the Lone Ranger, nor an
avenging angel. He belonged to a police force and did what he
was told. Still, with any luck he would not need to see the
preacher again to explain his inertia. And, God, did it matter a
bugger, anyway, what the smarmy-voiced little razor thought?
So he wore a brilliant bit of suiting. What could that do for
him? Sod all.

Harpur turned his brain towards sorting out where the leak
in Lloyd's had originated. Barton was keen on this, especially
if the treachery had come from the raided branch. Such foul-
ness on his own doorstep infuriated the Chief. It soiled the
town. Good Lord, he might have played bowls with the man
and might play with him again. He had to be nailed. Barton's
peers at the lodge and around those grim suburban pubs he
liked must be ribbing him about the mole. Some of them might
even have their loot in that very branch.

Possibly because of Barton's enthusiasm, Harpur found this
part of things a bore. Normally he would have enjoyed doing
what he could to take bank executives to pieces, and the place
was full of very promising tit who might reasonably be brought
into any inquiry, too. Just the same, Harpur left most of this
early stuff to Garland. He was wily, tough, arrogant – in fact,
man of the bloody match for arrogance – and would scare the
daylight and maybe bits of the truth out of the top lot at the
bank. Harpur could come in later on, when Garland had a

short-list. That's how it was at the top. You kept a dog and did not bark yourself, not until the barking meant you'd landed some bugger. Yes, a true art, leadership.

Twice he had reports that Mrs Avery was on the prowl again in whore streets at The Valencia, still buttonholing people, now obviously on the lookout for information about her husband's death. For her, searching like this or doing anything might be a bit of a therapy, and at first Harpur stayed clear, only telling patrols to keep an eye when they had time. At nearly 2 a.m. on the second night neighbours rang the local police to say the Avery children seemed unattended and were kicking up a din. Eventually the message reached Harpur, at home, awake in bed. He told them to send a WPC to the house, dressed, token listened to Megan beefing about being disturbed, and then took a car cruise around The Valencia.

He liked the idea of Ruth Avery digging. You could never tell, she just might bring something out, and if it gave a real, straight pointer to Avery's killers the Chief would have to ditch his grand policy of fuck-all and blind-eye, and make a move. The thing was, although Barton could order Harpur to forget Holly he could not control Ruth Avery. Harpur had always liked her toughness and fire; here they were being used for something bigger than sex games. She had so much fight it gave him a boost – and made him ashamed because it came new and not pleasant to be shown how to do your job by somebody's widow. She was taking on risks that should not have been necessary. If she asked questions in these streets the word would be around fast, but fast, and would reach Holly. Since the raid he had gone out of sight, but no question he would be comfy somewhere in London, with decent lines of communication. He might decide Ruth was like her husband, someone he would be better off without.

It took Harpur a while to find her tonight. The pair of plain-clothes men watching her off and on had answered a radio shout to a robbery earlier, and when they returned could no longer see Mrs Avery on the street. She might be on her way home, but Harpur doubted it. He thought for a while and then drove towards the abandoned house where Pablo the Pocket had been found. It was the longest of long shots, but she would have read of that in the papers and might know the connection with her husband.

Harpur entered the house through the same window as last time. From somewhere deep inside he heard a quavering, deeply pissed, but coherent male voice in a long, uninterrupted drone, like someone reciting – say, James Mason doing that slab from the Bible in *Odd Man Out*, but without the energy and blarney ham. From another part of the black interior came different voices, more men, in what could be a rambling, half-soaked argument. Did *The Tatler* know about the richness of night-life in The Valencia? He paused and swept the beam of his flashlight around but saw nothing, then moved on, stepping towards the recitation, and in a couple of minutes reached the room where the Pocket had been found. Now he could sort out the words being spoken.

> Where's the maid
> Whose lip mature is ever new?
> Where's the eye, however blue,
> Doth not weary? Where's the face
> One would meet in every place?
> Where's the voice, however soft,
> One would hear so very oft?
> At a touch sweet Pleasure melteth
> Like to bubbles when rain pelteth.
> Let them winged Fancy find
> Thee a mistress to thy mind.

There was a pause and then the voice snarled, 'Just a mind's eye girlfriend. What was Keats, a bloody wanker?'

Harpur swung the light again. The wino he had found here last time was on his feet tonight and wearing the filthy, beautifully cut overcoat that had been hanging up on the earlier visit. Though it was very warm, he had the coat buttoned to the chest and the collar up. Troubled by the torch beam the man made a half-turn away, continuing to spout the poem, occasionally raising an arm for emphasis. An open wine bottle stood a dozen yards from him alongside an old-style heavy suit-case covered in labels. Harpur moved the light off him and bit by bit illuminated the rest of the room.

It was then he found Ruth Avery. She was sitting on the floor and swiftly put up a hand to protect her eyes. For a moment she looked very frightened and Harpur suddenly realized that to her he was just an invisible newcomer, someone who might bring menace. The poetry man she must have come to regard as safe, part of the interior decor, but now here was someone extra and alien. Harpur watched her, tried to sort out why in the name of God she was here. Almost it looked as if she had settled down like one of the regular squatting dead-beats. Perhaps she had wanted to talk to the dross in here, see what she could discover about the day the Pocket got his, and instead was being given a slab of the *Golden Treasury*. Harpur's boys had questioned everyone in this house and he could have forewarned her that they knew nothing, but he doubted whether that would have worked. She had to do her own questioning and search. He could understand that. Why should she trust him or any other police to turn up the truth and do something with it?

'Ruth.'

'Mr Harpur? You won't find anything here. I've asked.'

'I was looking for you.'

'What made you think I'd be here? You a detective or some-bloody-thing?'

He heard the sound of hurried footsteps through the debris and when he moved the torch beam found the man in the over-coat had returned to his bottle, able to locate it in the dark by smell or love. He picked it up, held it against his chest like a mad woman with a doll as baby, but did not drink yet. Maybe he had simply been scared that this intruder would help himself; or it might be he still had a trace of middle-class delicacy and could not swig under a spotlight. When Harpur shifted the beam again he found Ruth Avery had stood up and was brushing muck from her jeans. In this he would not have minded helping, but held back. The side of her forehead was cut and more dust streaked her face and neck. Had she fallen? 'My friend, Julian, has been very kind,' she said. 'Not just the poems, but looking after me. The people upstairs are unpredictable, but he's a sweetie.'

The stupid, boudoir word used about this smelly wreck with his bottle and roughed-up liver somehow enraged Harpur, made him feel like an outsider, a nobody. Christ, did Ruth fancy this sad piece of work? She sounded comfortable here, as if at home among neighbours, some nice, some not, but a community. Shock must have knocked a hole in her mind to make her talk and behave like this. If he did not do something smartly she could become a long-term derelict herself. Grief changed people. Again he felt himself being pushed, required by self-respect to promise something, something big, something that would put things right. 'I know a few things already,' he said. 'I mean, about Brian.' It was coy, it was feeble. Even now, when he had seen how things were going to be, and when he longed to interest Ruth enough to draw her away from here, the usual copper's caginess operated.

'Well, I should hope you do know something.'

'Come on, Ruth, you ought to go home.'

'No hurry. What is it that you know? Tell me exactly. Some link?'

'Yes, a link.'

'A good one?'

'Very good. But let's go, Ruth.'

'Where?'

'It's too late to do anything tonight.'

'Of course it isn't. Night and day – all the same to police. They like visiting in the small hours, don't they? Makes things easier – people half asleep, no clothes, no shoes for running or kicking. If you've got something, let's act right now. In the morning you'll be damn different, I'd bet on it.' Yes, he might have bet on it, too. 'The shadow of Mr Barton will fall on you.'

Sharp. In one way she seemed very calm and rational. But was it sane to be calm and rational in such a setting? They stood facing each other in this waste of a place, the torch beam playing on the rubbish and broken glass between them, the poetry man quiet now and standing at the edge of the patch of light, apparently gazing into the dark at the far end of the room. At times as her words flowed he wondered whether someone had given her a snort of something good during her wanderings down here. Perhaps it wasn't shock but my lady snow.

'You weren't just talking big, were you?' she asked. 'Copper's talk?'

He thought of the preacher again, and his similar doubts. Was Harpur really becoming Mr Bullshit? 'I know who's behind the deaths.'

'Holly? Everyone's on to that. But how to get him?'

'I can do it.'

'How?'

Harpur glanced towards the Spirit of Poetry.

'He's on my side. He wouldn't talk,' she said.

Only if it rhymed. 'He doesn't know when he's talking. I can't say anything here.'

'All right, we'll go. That's what you want, yes?'

He put out a hand to help her and she ignored it.

'We'll go to whatever, whoever, you say is the link to Holly and then afterwards you can get the sod, can't you? There'll be nothing to stop you. In fact, you'll have to go. Police have duties, correct me if I'm wrong. If I've been a witness to it, Barton and Iles won't be able to put the stopper on, will they?' She was more or less speaking his own thoughts. 'Good-bye, Julian, love. Try not to overdo it. I have to go. This is very important business.'

'Let's see if you can get *Paradise Lost* off by heart before we're here next,' Harpur said. Then he took her out to the Ernest Bevin estate and Michael Martin Allen's place. When in doubt lean on an old lag. Allen was used to being knocked up at all hours and put through the mincer. In any case, he really was the route this time. He linked to Holly, no question.

Allen answered the door wearing a grey and gold silk dressing-gown, like something from a bloody awful early David Niven picture. Harpur had not seen it when he turned the place over, so Allen must have landed some cash. 'Where's the ciggy holder, Mike?'

'Ah, I thought it might be you, Mr Harpur.' In his crumby way Allen seemed almost poised, despite the time. Harpur found it unnerving. Suddenly he did not feel in command here. 'And a lady cop, too. That's very nice, but unusual. I'm glad you come. I had a message to get in touch with you. Come on in, both.'

The three of them stood crowded together in the little hall, Harpur jammed against a bamboo coat-stand that looked about strong enough to take a coolie hat.

'Rex Holly, who I think you know, asked me to fix up a meeting between you and him, personal, just the two of you,' Allen said.

Wrongfooted, baffled, Harpur could say only, 'Yes?' Christ, he had come here expecting a big show of ignorance and all the usual obstructiveness from Allen, and now here was Holly on a plate.

'This is good, isn't it?' Ruth Avery asked.

'Of course it's good, love,' Allen replied. 'The two big boys together.'

'What's it all about, Mike?' Harpur said.

'He got in mind a sort of deal. That's how I understand it.'

'What sort of deal?'

'Oh, police are always doing deals, aren't they? Give and take. Behind the scenes – trade-offs. That's the sort of thing.'

'He hasn't got anything to trade.'

'Well, I don't know about that. I'm only the go-between, Mr Harpur. But he seemed to think, yes, he got something, you see. Anyway, you can meet him and find what's what, can't you? And I told him you was the kind of man who would play it fair. I give my word on that. I said I knew you and I could swear that if you said it would be straight it would be straight, no men hiding round the corner to make a pounce, if there was anything to pounce on him for, I mean.'

Allen providing him with a reference: Jesus!

'So will you go?' Ruth asked.

'Of course he will, love.'

Harpur felt a touch of menace. It was in Allen's voice; it was in the idea of a deal and a trade. Was he in their power some-how, Allen's and Holly's?

'Rex knows you want the people who did one of your boys.'

'Too fucking true,' Ruth muttered. 'That's my man.'

'Oh, pardon me,' Allen said, 'I thought you was – Well, then, you can see what we're getting at. Mr Holly is ready to help on this.'

'Help? How the hell can he help?' she snarled.

'So what about it, Mr Harpur?'

They both stared at him. 'Yes,' he said.

'Alone?' Allen checked.

'Yes.'

'No colleagues to be informed even.'

'I understand.'

'Good, good. I think you'll be pleased, Mr Harpur. I mean, as long as you can go some way to meet him, the terms, that is. Give and take. I'll certainly pass the word on that you're ready and willing. Then I'll hear when and where. That's how it works. Could you be in touch here again? Give me a ring. No need to call, though you're always welcome, of course, both.'

'I'll phone tomorrow evening.' He thought of the last time he had been here, when Allen had gibbered and broken and talked about the hideout and the men he had shown around the town and briefed. Why did the bugger suddenly feel so safe? Had he forgotten all that, and the Leicas? Buy a new dressing-gown and transform your ego.

Allen grew solemn. 'Mrs Avery, I'd like to say how sorry I am about your husband. And I know Mr Holly feels – '

'Stuff it,' Harpur said, pushing him out of the way to leave. 'Just do what you have to.'

In the car, before they had moved off, she leaned across and kissed him very briefly on the cheek. When he turned, ready for anything, even here outside Allen's flat and in the middle of the Ernest Bevin, she was sitting upright again, fixing her seat-belt and gazing ahead. 'You'll pull Holly in, won't you?' she said. 'Such a turn up. Deals? Give and bloody take! Like you said, what's he got to offer? You just smash him, don't you? They always go too far. Brian used to say that. It's what gives the police their chance.'

He would have liked to think things with Holly were so simple, but on their way to her house he said nothing to undo her optimism. Enough pain had run her way, and he could not bear to hurt her more. It was nearly 3.30 a.m., when people could be near their lowest, yet Ruth sounded almost joyful. Let it stay like that for a while, at least. At her house she left the car at once, without any more signs of warmth. Those had to come from her or not at all. You did not stalk your colleague's widow so soon after his death. Later, things might be different.

16

Harpur did not play it quite straight, but then neither did Holly. In this sort of deal you had to allow yourself flexibility. Working in grey areas you used words in a way that lacked the solidity and sureness of the Book of Proverbs. Although there were villains Harpur would have agreed to meet one-to-one and actually gone to meet one-to-one, Holly was not among them. He was too big to do things alone and too big to speak the whole truth. It could be that Harpur might decide to pull Holly in, and if that happened and Holly had a battalion hidden nearby there would be difficulties.

So Harpur took Francis Garland. There could still be difficulties. Although he might dispute it, Garland was only one. They would not be armed, because the meeting was clandestine and Harpur could give no reason for an issue of guns. Besides, the venue picked by Holly, and skilfully picked, was a street likely to be packed with the fairly innocent at the time of their meeting, and it would be dangerous for Harpur and Garland to fire. Police had to bother about such things, though Holly did not.

The message that came from Allen when Harpur rang was that Rex thought the 'conference' should be on some neutral

116

ground, a half-way point. 'He realizes you wouldn't want to go to London on his patch, Mr Harpur, and he don't want to come here. So he asks, what about Birmingham?'

'But where else? A hotel room? Safe house?'

'No, Rex don't like enclosed spaces.'

Tough. Holly was going to finish in one, either brick or wood.

'Make a real outing of it, he says, Mr Harpur. There's an open-air market every Saturday morning in Birmingham at the Rotunda – a big ugly brown church close by. Rex's view is that this would be suitable, watch how the other half lives, like. Next Saturday. About 11 a.m.?'

'Rain or shine?'

'He's pretty lucky. I wouldn't be surprised if the sun comes out for him.'

'He's lucky all right.' It would do. Harpur might have preferred a room or a building, for all the reasons that Holly feared. With someone between walls, you were half-way to holding him. Why bloody Birmingham? Did he have an outpost of heavies there, or a good bolt-hole nearby if things did turn out messy? 'It's on.'

For the trip Garland dressed to look like what he pictured as the typical bottom-grade Brummie shopper, Littlewoods cardigan, jeans, sandles, Littlewoods shirt, open, with a St Somebody medallion in genuine metal. He would pick up a local carrier-bag and items to go in it when they arrived. Garland always said he could lose himself in any background except a conference of jockeys or Labour Party women. In the car he started to ask questions about the meeting, but was bright enough to know when to stop, which was one reason Harpur had chosen him.

'You're going just for a talk?'

'That's it.'

'And you'll stick to that as a limit.'

'Probably. See what he has to say.'

'He could disappear again. Do you want me to try to tail him after?'

'It's not on. We're in the middle of a Saturday city. Crowds.

In and out of shops. He's picked the place well.'

'I could try.'

'It's not worth it. Don't worry. We're in touch through Allen.'

'For as long as Holly wants that.'

Obviously true, but Harpur had had enough and did not reply. What was there to say – that Holly must be handled carefully because he had relayed a mysterious threat or two? Garland read the silence right and settled back for a doze. He had been going at the work hard in the bank and also might have fixed himself up with one of the nice range of girl clerks there, an extra call on his sap.

As Allen had promised, the sun put on a good show for the meeting and it looked as if Garland, in his beige and yellow manmade-fibre cardigan, might appear overdressed. The world wore a T-shirt today, even Holly, and most of the world seemed to be here, buying plastic shoes and ready-to-hang pelmets off the barrows.

Holly was loitering near a baby-clothes display, on his features a small, wholesome smile, perhaps an attempt to look fatherly. Through the crowd Harpur watched him for a second or two and tried to pick out his support among the shoppers. They would be in jackets, because you couldn't hide a gun in a T-shirt, and Harpur studied a couple of wiry men wearing summer suits and scanning old paperbacks on offer at 10p each behind the baby-clothes stall. The tailoring and haircuts looked sharp for Birmingham, but who knew what Britain's second city was capable of these days? Did people who could put out that much on suits and coiffures buy second-hand paperbacks? He would have liked to see their faces, but they seemed very preoccupied with the literature and kept their backs to him, seemingly not interested in what was behind them: they might know a thing or two about surveillance techniques.

Harpur could not delay long. The chances were that he had already been seen, although Holly had not seemed to look his way either. Garland would have arrived here five minutes earlier and be somewhere among the sweltering, not-too-pretty crowd. Harpur wished he could spot him.

'I'm Harpur.'

'Of course you are. Shall we stroll?' A clown on stilts crossed ahead of them towards a children's play area. 'Plenty of life here. Who said Britain was in a terminal doze?'

'I'd have recognized you anywhere, with or without a mask.'

'My mother always said I had a distinctive physique – finely made yet full of strength and energy. Like Diaghilev.'

'They say he was so supple he could suck his own cock.'

'On stage? Let's look at these, shall we?' He stopped at a stall of framed, mass-produced pictures, the raindrop on a rose, a man's best friend bringing his slippers, all the usual gleaming crap. 'Art, I could wallow in it, couldn't you, Mr Harpur?'

'Cheese is my weakness, like Ben Gunn.'

His head came up very sharply. Perhaps he had heard 'Bren Gun'. Then he turned back to the pictures. 'You could be used to a nicer class of product, of course.'

Harpur thought he began to see the drift.

They walked again, edging their way between the shoppers. He spotted the two men in summer suits, still not far off, still with their backs to him as they appeared to study curtain cloth now.

'I've had a business set-back lately,' Holly said. 'At the time it was very puzzling. But I've done some study on it since, a good deal of analysis and inquiring. That's how we behave in business, have to, if we're to survive. And I'm glad to say all the effort paid off. Do you know a man called Jack Lamb, Mr Harpur? But of course you do. I found he was the one who had caused my problems. Jack Lamb is well into art, you know. Of course you do. As I understand it from my inquiries, he can rely on pretty good cooperation from you as regards his art deals, and other things, too. It could be regarded as a kind of partnership, you and him.'

Yes, it could be, by an anti-police jury – and what other sort was there these days? The shape of the deal grew clearer and more painful. There would be no arrest of Holly here today, no arrest ever. An arrest meant a charge, and a charge meant

119

court. Court meant evidence, from both sides and Harpur could not risk that.

As if aware that some sort of new understanding had been formed, Holly said: 'We don't need to flog around these fucking stalls any longer. Let's go to a bar I know near here. I'll tell you what I'm proposing. If you're not mad you'll like it, Harpur.' He had dropped the voice of smarmy threat, his Peter Lorre take-off, and switched to normal – the rough-edged half-cockney of a thug with education. The dossier said a couple of years at Lancing or a place like that, and earlier a first-class prep school. He looked like the Scrubs now more than Lancing, but you could still pick out a bit of refinement in his face, a touch of privilege.

They went to the restaurant bar of the Midland Hotel.

'Hattersley eats here,' Holly said.

'Diaghilev, Hattersley. You're a name-dropper.' Harpur hated to think of his own name on the lips of this bastard. Holly should be able to get a laugh out of telling how he tied up this big copper from Hicksville and got him to forget a few little things like the torture and murder of one of his mates and the killing of his nark. For a second, Harpur was close to grabbing him by his monogrammed T-shirt and taking the bugger in, let Barton and Iles make what the hell they liked of it. He resisted that surge of loony hate, though, and it withered. Good impulses often did.

For Holly to propose coming inside must mean he felt safe now that he had disclosed what he knew and shown the damage he could do. They took a table near an open window and just before he sat down Harpur saw Garland on the pavement outside, his carrier bag bulging. He must have followed them and would be wondering about his next move. Holly leaned forward and spoke swiftly and quietly. 'I can give you the men who did Avery and your Sambo grass, the men and enough forensic for you to nail them good.'

'These are – '

'We're fixing a deal, right? Let's leave everything else out of it. Look, I don't give a shit what you think of me. OK, it's dirty, I don't say anything different. They're my own people, yes, but I've got to do what I can to save myself, haven't I? That's what it's all about. Their families will be looked after.' He sipped his Coke and sat back, pale and sweating some, but he would not die of shame. 'That's my offer, plus no noise from me about the arrangement of yours with Jack Lamb on the crooked art. The press would love that, but I'm silent for ever if we come to an agreement. So, what do I want from you?'

'Your neck. Immunity.'

'One, stop trying to fit me into the Lloyd's job. Two, stop believing I was behind what happened to Avery and the coon. The quiet life, that's all I'm asking you for. Leave me alone. Look, I get reports that this wouldn't be difficult, not at all difficult. Your Chief doesn't want to push things against yours truly. But it's you who keeps on having a chew at the situation. All right, I can understand it – a colleague, a special grass. Of course you dig away. And, then again, you've got people inside who could do me damage, and you hammer them for a statement. But if you want this deal you must knock it all off as of now, you savvy? Just do what your bosses tell you, play it easy. You could get me twenty years. Maybe that's what you want. Well, too bad. If I'm in trouble you're in trouble with me. That's the score.'

Holly's information was good but a long way from good enough. Pray God it stayed like that. If he ever discovered that the Chief and Iles were not just lukewarm about hunting him but dead against, Harpur would have nothing to offer in a deal. Garland entered the bar and sat down on the other side of the room, not seeming to notice them. He began to do an inventory of his packages.

'How do you see it?' Holly said.

'What forensic?' He thought he sensed movement at the back of the big dining-room which adjoined the bar, but saw nothing.

'Clothes mainly. Blood traces. This is not rubbish, not a frame. These boys really did it.'

'Because you told them to. They might sing in court.'

'I doubt it. I told you – they've got families. They know the sort of game they're in in. Big money if it goes all right, shit flying if not. I said they were my people, which is half right. They're hired for a job, and that's the end of it. Not family. No big-time loyalties involved. They knew from the start they could end up carrying the can.'

Holly put down his glass, preparing to leave. 'I know you're not buyable, Harpur – with cash, I mean, so I have to offer something else and this is it. It's got to be bloody barter, hasn't it? I don't make a habit of giving my boys away, but what else?' He leaned forward even closer. 'Don't want your sidekick to hear this,' he muttered, indicating Garland by a movement of his head, 'but my reports say you are sniffing around the Avery widow, might already have got there, in fact. Why all the aggro, then? Haven't we done you a bit of service, seeing off the competition?'

This time Harpur did grab him, but by the hair, yanking his head hard down so his face cracked beautifully on the rim of the Coke glass, shattering it. Blood gushed from half a dozen spots in a perfect circle from the bridge of his nose to his chin, and the barman uttered an excited yelp. Garland stood up. The two men in summer suits appeared from the shadows of the dining-room and came swiftly towards Harpur. He released Holly and got up to face them. Behind, the barman mewed. Garland crossed the room and took a spot alongside Harpur.

'It's all right,' Holly muttered, still seated. 'I'm not bad, not bad at all. An accident. Leave him, Sandy, Doug. A napkin?' he called to the barman. 'No need to send for anyone, I'll be fine.' The barman brought a cloth and he wiped his face. 'Is it on then?' he asked Harpur, in as near a normal voice as he could do. The stiff upper lip was one feature not cut.

'It's got to be, hasn't it?' Harpur had enjoyed that. For a while Holly had looked like the left-overs from a tap-room brawl, not someone with a bit of upbringing and cash.

In the car Garland asked what the hell had gone on. 'If there's one thing I hate it's insults that get near the truth,' Harpur replied.

When they were back he called Lamb and fixed an immediate

meeting. They sometimes used the car-park of a late opening hypermarket and Harpur decided this would do today, though he never much liked it: what were they supposed to be doing, two big men in the front of a car, surrounded by shoppers and their loaded trolleys but not shopping?

Jack used to say, 'We could be waiting for our women.'

'We could be jerking each other off. We'll have the vice boys dropping on us one day.'

But tonight he could not waste time trying to think of new venues. In any case, what he had to say to Jack would not take long. 'It's happened. Holly's got you spotted, Jack.'

He must have lived with the possibility since the first tip about Lloyd's, and he took it calmly enough now.

'I'm not in a position to give you protection,' Harpur said.

He guffawed. 'What kind of dead-beat language is that for an old mate? "Not in a position to offer protection." Jesus.'

'OK, I *can't*. If I ask for men for you I've got to say how I know you're in danger, and that's not on.'

'Would I take protection if you could offer it, Col? Would it be half-way efficient if you could, Col?' He laughed again. 'Don't bloody fret so much. You're full of doom, always have been. Something dark and Germanic in your nature. Where's your family tree got its roots?'

'You might be safe. I've got a deal with him. If he goes through with it, you're probably OK.'

They were in Lamb's big Vauxhall. He could just get behind the wheel. 'I don't like to hear of you negotiating with rubbish like Holly.'

'That's the game I'm in. If it wasn't Holly it would be someone else. The world's full of rubbish.'

'But he might not keep the deal? That figures, with this slippery sod.'

'There was a bit of unpleasantness at the end of our discussion. It could have alienated him. But he didn't say so. In fact, the opposite.'

'What kind of deal?'

'Where's the art?'

'Pollock and Rossetti? Still got them. The women like the

123

paintings so much, not just Fay, but mother. She's still over here. I don't want to upset her; I'm a softie like that. Thought I might look around for a buyer when she goes back after another couple of months.'

'You ought to shift them.'

'Do they come into all this? He knows about them?'

'Something like that.'

'I see.' Lamb nodded his huge head a couple of times, marking off in his mind the ways the situation had changed. 'So, if the deal goes wrong he might come hunting me and do for you by showing you knew about the pictures.'

'Can you get abroad for a while?'

'You asked that before. Do a runner? It's a bit feeble. And I'd have to sell the art in a hurry. I couldn't leave it, could I? That's not the way to do these things, rush them. I might lose a packet. And mother's gone to some relations in Wales for a while; I wouldn't like her to come back to my place and find I'd flogged them while she was absent, and then scarpered. How could I go, anyway, while she's still in Britain? I can't leave her alone here. Holly's a specialist on family connections, isn't he? As it happens, that's why I owed him something. Did I ever tell you? Possibly not. It hurts. A long time ago he wanted to get at me over some disagreement we'd had and he arranged for my wife to walk into what looked like your run-of-the-mill muggers, except that the beating was so expert she died. The Met never got close, of course. They told me a woman shouldn't be out walking alone.'

'So maybe he'll have you mugged next?'

'He might try.' Lamb left the car and helped a woman reload a trolley she had managed to capsize. Returning he said: 'We could be panicking, couldn't we Col? Do I read the situation right? As far as we know, the deal is on. If so, we're both in the clear.'

'I wanted to warn you.'

'Yes, thanks. And you're worried about that glittering super-cop career.'

'A bit.'

'So do you really want me to get rid of the merchandise at

124

any price? I'll do it if you say so. I could make it up somehow to the women.'

Harpur felt ashamed again. 'No, let's trust the little runt, shall we? See how it goes.'

'Good, Col. I hate to see you sweating over small things.'

'Do you carry any armament these days, Jack?'

He ignored that. 'What about an address for Holly?'

'No chance.'

'Well, some chance. I might make an inquiry or two.'

'For what?'

'Col, I hate being on the defensive.'

'Now listen – don't shove your neck into something. He'll know you might try.'

'See you soon, then. We'll get you to Chief Constable yet.'

'Jack, was that true about your wife?'

17

A couple of days later when he arrived home in the early evening, Harpur's younger daughter Jill said, 'Someone's been hanging about waiting to see you.' She did not take her eyes from a boxing programme on television. 'He looks like a habitual criminal.' From the age of seven she had been a phrasemaker, had picked up the talent from her mother.

'Waiting where?'

'Hanging about just at the corner. You can see him from the window upstairs.'

'How do you know he's waiting for me?' Harpur said, sitting down with her.

'I don't,' she said wearily. 'It was how he looked. I made a guess. And there's a dirty blue van. All right?' She seemed to think the van clinched it, and it did, though she could not know that.

'I shouldn't think he wants me.'

She shrugged. That might be the end of it as far as she was

concerned. Then after a while she said in a commercial break, 'He was looking pretty jumpy.'

'Fed up with waiting, you mean?'

'Jumpy.'

It could only be Michael Martin Allen, and Harpur grew jumpy himself, but he stuck at the show of calm and the interrogation. 'Tell me exactly, Jill, what connected him in your mind with me.'

'Oh, God, the third degree. I told you, he's a slug in a suit and he holds a cigarette like he has to hide it, the way they do inside. But forget it. It was a feeling, but like I say – '

'As I say.'

'As I say, forget it if you like – or should it be, forget it if you as? I thought you'd be interested, that's all.'

There were not many maxims he lived by but one was, never let your children see you anxious. Harpur set his chair to face away from the boxing and read the local paper which said the Home Secretary had appointed a senior officer from another force to look into the Lloyd's incident. A couple of Labour MPs were reported as doing the standard stuff about public dissatisfaction with a procedure which allowed police to investigate police. The public did not have a single thought on it. Only a copper and a crook were killed, no babies or dogs. Who bothered? It would be a pain, going through all that rigmarole, fielding questions for once instead of asking them, and sitting there while some scribe longhanded it all for signature. He should have fired first, that was the long and short of it, and the inquiry might say so. If he had, of course, there would still have been an inquiry and the report would then have said he had been hasty. But at least Peters would be still alive. And Holly might well have been inside and safe but for those few moments of delay while they tended Peters. Yes, next time, if it came, he would try to arrange things so he shouted 'Armed police' and fired at the same time. That would satisfy everyone except the man who stopped the bullet.

When her programme ended Jill left the house to play, and as soon as she had gone he walked up the street towards

Allen's van. Nearby a gang of youngsters, black and white, girls and boys, loitered around a couple of motorbikes, Jill not among them as far as he could make out, nor Hazel her sister. He climbed into the cab. 'Drive somewhere. Anywhere.'

He had on the shagged-out brown suit. 'Sorry if I've done something out of turn coming here, Mr Harpur.' He did not sound it. That new lurid cockiness still fizzed. This dead-beat really thought he was getting somewhere, and somewhere without bars on the window. 'Rex has had some second thoughts. He asked me to pass on a few new terms to the agreement, what's known as "amendments" in business. That's why I come urgent – I knew it must be important. That your daughter, in and out of the upstairs room, looking from the window just now?'

'Why?'

'Nice kid. I seen her come home from school and go out again.'

'You can't be trying to say what I think you are.'

'What's that, Mr Harpur? Don't get ratty. There's no glass for me to fall on here.'

'Always remember, Mike, you're a small-time bum who might, with big luck, climb to being an arsehole. Any time I like I can have you stuck away for fifteen. When you threaten me or my family you're – '

'Would I threaten? Can't a man make a remark?'

'Not just gaol. How would it be if I let Holly know you considerately pointed me towards the William Walton bolt-hole?' They pulled in at a park and walked like a couple of friends.

'I hadn't realized what you done to Rex, you see,' Allen said. 'I heard violence, but not a glassing. What kind of officer does that?'

'He was trying to nut me, and missed. I've got a witness.'

'He needs plastic surgery. It's made him very hard towards you, very mean.'

'Oh, dear.'

'I don't know the details of your deal, you understand. All I got to do is pass on what he said. What he says is, he has found out since he talked to you in Birmingham what your bosses think about trying to do him, and it's not just they're not keen, they won't have it at any price. So, he thinks this makes his position pretty strong. You can't do nothink to him, so why should he worry? But he's going to stick to the deal, never mind the terrible injuries to his face and never mind your Chief. Rex says when a businessman makes a deal he got to abide by it, because if there is no trust the whole system will collapse.'

'How true.'

'What he says is to call off Mr Francis Garland from the inquiries he's doing at the bank.'

Because the inside man could name Holly as his contact. 'That won't be too easy.'

'Can't you tell him to say he can't find anything so he's giving up? You police, you can arrange things. You're doing it all the time – who gets done, who doesn't. Who knows who, that's the thing, isn't it? I never knew nobody, so I was always getting put away. Now it's a bit different, I work for Mr. Holly. I'm not on my own any more, not a bloody soft target for your boys. You knows it goes on. So, just tell him to ease up at Lloyd's, not to try so hard, don't ask too many questions. He got to do what you say, yes?'

They didn't know Garland. 'What else did Holly say?'

'Well, there *is* something else. How did you know? You're a smart one.'

Women in whites were playing a bowls match, and they stopped and watched. This was one of the Chief's games. It quietened his soul, he said.

'There's always something else in – ' Harpur had been going to say in blackmail. That might make Allen feel even better and more powerful, if he did not already know Holly had a hold. So he ended, ' – in dealing with someone like Holly.'

'It's because he's so angry over your attack on him, what he's right to call defacement.'

'Defacement happens to walls.'

'He's got appearances to keep up. It's important.'

128

'He feels self-conscious when he walks into White's?'

'White's what?'

'Go on. What else?'

'He says that Mr Jack Lamb has some valuable material that he and you both knows about. I've heard of Jack Lamb. I only just found out that you and him – Anyway, don't ask me what these valuable things are but he says you'll cotton on, immediate. Well, they got to be handed over to him – he says to help make up for what he lost because of Mr Lamb not long ago. Don't ask me what that means either. All I am is the messenger.'

Harpur would never have forecast this demand. Did Holly know the first tiny thing about trading in pictures? His doctorate was on 'The Effects of Sprayed Ammonia on the Human Eye', not the Impressionists. It would be dangerous for him to hold these paintings and to try and find the kind of specialist fence needed. But obviously he did not care, as long as he could cause a bit of pain to Lamb and Harpur, work a bit more revenge.

On the green a couple of the bowlers had begun pushing each other and shouting about a disputed measurement from the jack. Three or four more of these heavily built, elderly, beautifully turned out players joined in and there was some kicking. Other women tried to break it up. An aged park-keeper hobbled warily towards them. Men's bowls obviously were not like this, or Barton couldn't take the pace.

They turned back towards the van. 'Drop me at a taxi stand,' Harpur said.

'You don't like being with someone like me, do you? Jack Lamb, yes.' With the cockiness seemed to have come a new intensity and the ability to express himself. 'You know what I mean, Mr Harpur. You don't like messing about with what you think of as little people. I used to be one – scratching a little living, half the time inside, half the time living in some dump on the Ernest Bevin. You can get after them, can't you, because they're weak, no big lawyers, no big mates, no luck. They can't frighten you and your sort. They got to wait for you to call, like a dose of the 'flu, and they don't kick. It's like they was doomed and they knows it. They don't make a song if you turn your big-boot squads over their houses and mess up their stuff. That's life, for them.'

It came close, bloody close, and Harpur was silent.

'Then you got someone like Jack Lamb, into all the big rackets, all of them pulling in more in a year than I could make in ten. Never pushed about by the cops, treated like a king. He's so crooked he's met himself coming back, haven't he, and got nearly respectable. As long as he don't strangle you or rape your daughter, he's in the clear, right? Mr Holly is the same, isn't he – too big for you? OK, so you gets heavy with him once in a while, but you can't really touch him, can you? I mean, put him away.'

Trust Allen to go too far and muck it up. About Lamb he had it right. Of course, of course. Harpur wouldn't and couldn't touch him because the holy bonds of narkdom had lasted too long for that and were too powerful. But Holly? What Allen said about him was true, too, but only true to date, and that could be put right, had to be put right. What kind of life would it be to know that this little derelict thought the big derelict could do what he liked with Harpur? Oh, no, that had to be buried deep somehow, and soon.

'I'm going to bear it in mind, what Holly says,' he told Allen.

'Well, you bloody better.'

'Moved those Leicas yet?'

And then, suddenly, out of nowhere, the chance to deal with Holly, face him solo and finish him, presented itself to Harpur. Everything could be settled, above board and no awkward ends. There would be risk, big risk, but what else when you were looking for a one-to-one with Holly? Some risks were not just reasonable but a duty. They came with the rent allowance. Harpur found himself alight with excitement and fear, not stupid excitement and not crippling fear. He could handle them both. When he thought about it later, he could only compare the exhilaration with feelings that came years ago on hearing his first daughter had been safely delivered. Now, though, the thrill seemed to spring from the chance of a death, Holly's death at his hands. That was what he meant when he thought of finishing Holly – not nailing him for a court and thirty years, but knocking him off good. Harpur saw that he must be changing. Well, any job would shape you, work a few amendments, if you believed in it and stayed long enough to see what happened to the ones who came apart like Barton. Once in a while, 'shoot first' might be the right gospel.

It was Garland's work at the bank which produced the chance against Holly. From Lloyd's Garland reported that he would soon charge the voice, and had begun giving him a quota of harass. There had been three very long question sessions, one before the Birmingham visit, two since. Holly must get to know about these last two, and would be unhappy.

To break the leaking banker up some more, Garland had also organized a couple of anonymous abusive telephone calls and put him under round-the-clock watch, ordering the men doing it to be as heavy as they liked. A bank manager living in a nice road with patios and balconies would not like all that rough muscle with sideboards and shiny shoes ogling over the privet. His name was Cadoxton, a securities executive on the way to forty, fairly recently transferred to the town from Liverpool. He ran a newish Rover 3500, had three kids at private schools, and was contributing to domestic costs for what Garland described as a very fine slice of long-legged extra in the goy ghetto of Mill Hill. Even with his easy mortgage from the bank, he was at full stretch and more. Garland had the figures and they added up to too much. You could see why he might trade a whisper. He must be a lad with good ears for what was going on in parts of the bank outside his own corner. But then £4 million in cash would send out bonny signals to everyone stricken by a bad dose of debt and listening hard for Fate's get-well message.

One night, Garland had left to take out a girl from Lloyd's when the detective watching Cadoxton radioed in to say he had lost him, apparently on the way to some sort of secret meeting. Harpur was drinking in the club and they rang through to tell him. His excitement started at once. He saw a rich bucketful of possibilities. Taking a pistol, he drove out to meet the officer at the spot where Cadoxton had ditched him, an area of old factories and warehouses at the edge of The Valencia. 'He deliberately shook you off, Ray?'

'I know this district well, sir, but he knows it better.' The man was almost sobbing with remorse. 'He was out three times to a pay phone tonight. He must think we've got a tap on. It looks as if he made a rendezvous and was determined to keep it private.'

'What time – the calls?'

'Between 5.15 and 6 o'clock.'

'Hang on here. I might be able to stir him.' It must be on the cards that Cadoxton had come out to meet Holly. Cadoxton might have cracked under Garland's treatment and gone to demand help. Holly could easily have driven down from London in the four hours since the calls, but he would be here to silence Cadoxton, not aid him, now that Harpur was obviously not keeping his side of the deal. If it really was Holly, the swiftness of his departure from London could mean he had come alone. He would be armed. How else could he deal with Cadoxton?

To Harpur everything looked beautiful. He could not have planned it better. With a bit of luck Holly might try to turn the gun on Harpur, and Harpur could blast him, finish it sweetly, confer on him the kind of silence Holly wanted to give Cadoxton. That would please everyone – himself, Lamb, Barton, Iles, even Cadoxton, if Harpur managed to save him. Christ, it had to be OK to pull a gun on a gun when two lives were at risk and one was a bank manager, bent or not. God, let Holly be armed and let him try it. Some childhood dread of blasphemy made him appalled for a moment that he had put the appeal for the chance to kill a man as a prayer. Yes, this case had done something to him, and he could not wait around to decide whether it was plus or minus.

This was the kind of operation best handled solo. No need

for them to look for Garland: a good cop never slept but was entitled to go to bed with a woman. It might cut some of the bugger's bounce, anyway, if he missed the big face-to-face. Harpur was the number one prodigy in this outfit and a pushy understudy could be a pain. Then there was the fact that he would prefer tonight not to have witnesses. Any report for Barton and Iles would come from him and only from him. Or, if things went badly for Harpur, there would be no report at all, only another ceremonial dress funeral for the two of them.

'There might be a gun around,' he told the tail. 'Play it very tight if I flush out someone you don't recognize, and don't put your head in the way of anything. Just get a good look for identification.'

'Do you want me to call aid, sir?'

'Not yet. It's only a guess. Cadoxton might be just tomcatting.'

He left the car and started walking. The tactics could be all balls, he knew that. Cadoxton might simply have brought the detective into this maze to drop him, and could be miles away by now. Wouldn't it be saner to put out a call for his car to be stopped? He might try that later. At the moment his excitement stayed solid and high. There could be something and something for him only. Whiz-kids needed to whiz often if they were to stay ahead. In any case, and just as important, this was a matter of protecting his arse. Holly was best silent, silenced.

Tonight, instinct and hope paid off and it took him only half an hour to find the Rover. The car had been driven into the courtyard of an abandoned warehouse and tucked in against a wall, so deeply shadowed that Harpur almost missed it. As the tail had said, it looked as if Cadoxton kept a map of this area in his head, and had used it previously for meetings.

The warehouse was open to the world – no doors, hardly a window. He went in, feeling at first that he was on a re-run of the day they found Pablo the Pocket near here in that Valencia house. Again he was walking on debris, breathing nauseating odours and again he carried a flashlight he feared to use. Here, though, there was no boarding up and half the roof had gone, so some moonlight entered, making things a bit easier. Here, too, of course, he had the .38. It was still in the holster but he kept one hand on it ready. There must be no more failures or freeze-ups as at Lloyd's. The media might go for his bollocks, but that was better than being knocked over. This revelation had been slow in coming but now he lived by it.

He was disappointed to have found only one car. Had Cadoxton really come for a meeting? Were two people present? He saw pretty soon that there was nobody at all on the ware-house ground-floor. At each end of the building was a square tower: there must have been an overhead crane here once. He began to mount the stone steps in one tower to what would once have been a control room at the top. It was hard going, and now and then he stopped to rest and to listen. Now he had very little moonlight and on the whole felt grateful for that because he would be less of a target from above.

At a landing half-way up he went into what had been an office of some kind in the old days, and through the windows could look down on the approaches to the warehouse from a different side. He saw what looked like main railway lines and a narrow footbridge over them, and as he gazed out he realized the mistake he had made. Searching the warehouse was an absurdity, no more than a repeat of that search for the Pocket. Because they had found someone there he had acted now as if every abandoned building was sure to produce. He had failed to think, had been programmed by a memory. Nobody sane would risk coming into such a black hole for a meeting.

He could make out far-off the gleam of another parked car, too distant to identify the make. There had been a rendezvous, all right, but not in here. Nearer now, a man suddenly appeared on the footbridge, running towards the warehouse and Harpur. Almost certainly it was Cadoxton. Immediately behind him came another man in pursuit, possibly Holly though about that Harpur was less sure. Almost at once the second man flung himself forward, arms stretched out to tackle, and both of them hit the floor. They stood again immediately, grappling with each other, and even at that distance Harpur thought he heard a shout or groan. Why this scrambling brawl? If it was Holly and he wanted to finish someone, wouldn't he use a bullet? Did he fear the noise? Had Cadoxton managed to disarm him somehow before this? After a few minutes he could no longer tell which man had been ahead, as they writhed and butted, punched and wrestled, all the time changing positions. It was like an out-of-focus stretch in some fancy film, with no sound now, or very little. Occasionally one or both would crash against the wall of the bridge and the noise reached Harpur, but he heard no more shouts or groans. They had to keep their strength and wind. Each would be frantic to stay on his feet and knew that the first to go to the ground again would never get up.

Harpur prepared to move. Could anyone lie low and watch a killing? Yes, he could have, if he had been sure Holly would be the one to go under. But Cadoxton was not a heavy, just a bank manager. Harpur would have to sort this out, and he began making his way as fast as he could down the steps. As he left the warehouse and ran towards the bridge he saw one of the men suddenly crash against the wall and then collapse, his body hopelessly, terrifyingly slack. At once the other began to put the boot in, slow, careful, merciless.

Harpur reached the footbridge and raced up the steps. At the top he saw the body on the floor and a man straightening from it, as if he had been throttling or knifing the motionless figure. Harpur yelled his 'Armed police' formula, but the man had heard him coming before that and turned now and bolted away towards the other end of the bridge and down the stairs at that end. Perhaps he thought there was a bit of an army on the way. Harpur shouted again, 'Holly, stop!' The name was a gamble, but a pretty safe one. He ran as hard as he could across the bridge, past the man on the floor. As soon as he could, he would come back to him, though it already looked too late. The face fitted Garland's descriptions of Cadoxton. All the time Harpur kept himself ready to go down fast and bring out the pistol.

He reached the steps at the other end and was about to

descend when he saw a small flash from below and heard the flat, short sound of a silenced pistol. A bullet tore into the handrail. Frenziedly he pulled back and crouched out of sight against the wall of the footbridge, drawing the Smith and Wesson. How the hell had he come to present himself like that, as bonny a target as anyone could hope for, framed in the entrance to the bridge? All he lacked was a fairground hat with *Kill Me Quick* written on it. For a second he must have stopped listening for the footsteps, had not noticed the man had paused. At the worst and most dangerous moment he had relaxed, like a kid cop, judgement blotted out and blood up in the excitement of a private vengeance chase. Jesus! His only excuse could be that he had come to believe there was no gun because it had not been used in the fight.

Completely flat on the filthy floor of the bridge, he edged forward to look around the corner and down the stairs. He had seen nothing of the man once he had left the bridge and still could not locate him. If he saw him, he would fire. He was entitled now – there had been a warning, and he had been shot at. They could dig the bloody shell out of the woodwork. Oh, Christ, for a sighting! He was not badly placed here, firing down on to the target, if he had a target. Once more he shouted, 'Holly, armed police. Give yourself up! You're surrounded!' He wanted to provoke another shot to help pinpoint him and ensure that Holly was still facing this way. What Harpur must not do was shoot him in the back. Tricky, very, to make that look like self-defence.

When next he heard something it came not from the darkness below but from behind him. He was suddenly aware of a slithering, lumbering sound and he turned his head to look while scrambling up quickly to get on guard. His first thought was that Holly had done a circle, and he swept the pistol around ready. The man he had passed on the floor, seemingly dead, was on his feet and making towards Harpur. His legs would hardly bear him and he advanced by leaning back against the footbridge wall and moving in small, careful steps sideways. Only a mighty exercise of will could have dredged up the strength. The strange rubbing sound that Harpur had heard was the friction of Cadoxton's jacket against the wall – if it was Cadoxton. His head hung forward and his arms were loose, and he looked like a boxer who had taken a hammering but was up again, supported by the ropes, apparently conscious of nothing except the need to move himself from this place and the best way, the only way, to do it.

If Harpur remained where he was this man would collide with him in a little while. Moving to the other side of the footbridge, Harpur watched him approach. The man stopped and his legs seemed about to give. His breathing was noisy, a rasping, gurgling sound, heavy with effort, the kind of desperate wheezing Harpur had heard from knife victims. Then he seemed to recover a little and began moving again.

In a while he stood almost opposite Harpur and became aware for the first time that someone else was present. He attempted to raise his head to look squarely at Harpur. Once more the effort was immense, a gradual, uncertain movement enabling him eventually to gaze straight ahead for a second before the neck muscles capitulated and his face sank forward. As his eyes met Harpur's the man made a small, cryptic gesture with one hand, a sideways action as if brushing something away, perhaps a sign to Harpur to be gone, maybe no more than an involuntary symptom of shock at finding someone else here. Harpur stepped towards him and put out a hand, fearing that in his strange, dogged progress Cadoxton would come to the end of the bridge without expecting it and pitch down the steps, or perhaps make himself the kind of helpless target that Harpur had just offered.

But this man did not look for kindness, perhaps no longer understood it, and as Harpur's fingers touched his shoulder he tried to slew away and began raising an arm, this time not to gesture but as if to strike the unknown hand from him. The effort was too much and he lost his balance. Harpur placed the flashlight down and put the pistol away, stepping nearer and grabbing at the man's jacket with both hands to stop him falling. At first he could manage the weight and held him easily. After a few seconds though the burden increased suddenly and he had to change his hold, taking him in a bear hug because the legs had finally given out. Cadoxton's arms fell back to his side and his body lost all strength. For a moment or two Harpur kept him upright, hoping for a recovery which did not come. The laboured breathing faltered and then seemed to peter out completely. In an attempt to rouse him Harpur began to talk, 'Cadoxton?' he said. 'Mr Cadoxton? Why are you here? Was it Holly? I'm a police officer. It's all right.' Not exactly. Gently Harpur lowered him to the floor and as he did saw that a little blood had oozed from Cadoxton's nose and mouth, smearing Harpur's sleeve and shirt-cuff. He laid him on his back and through Boy Scout's instinct, nothing more, loosened the tie and collar and even felt for a neck pulse, finding none nor expecting to.

Staring towards the top of the steps near him he realized these few moments had been full of peril. While struggling with this body he would have been easy pickings if the man from below had returned – and God knew there had been enough noise to draw him back, the gasps, the sliding feet. . . . Harpur listened, and from not too far away heard a car start and move off very fast. He pulled out the pistol again and rushed down the steps in time to hear the vehicle more clearly from somewhere behind an old foundry, but not to see it. He kept running, ready to open fire on the driver if there was a glimpse, and bugger the aftermath. There never was a glimpse though, only the dwindling sound of a big engine climbing to speed. He had an idea that all prospects for the deal went with that car. Holly had written it off, or why would he have needed to take risks removing Cadoxton? There would be no handing over of the men supposed to have done Avery and Paine and the Pocket. Holly had come to see that he was the only target Harpur cared about.

18

About the death of the bank mouth Barton might have been much worse. He seemed to have accepted that his last months in the job were heavily and unchangeably jinxed and now saw disaster after disaster as his lot. Iles, who would be left to pick up the pieces, was less philosophical, and accused Harpur to his face of botching things. Fair enough. Iles meant letting Cadoxton get killed, but for Harpur it was the survival of Holly that screamed failure. He could not fret about Cadoxton. The bank manager had chosen to run with people who played rough, and had to take what came.

From his soul's stockroom Barton had brought out a permanent, sad half-smile, which meant long-suffering and a readiness to forgive. 'We're going to have to call a press conference, Colin. A few selected, responsible journalists to whom we can be reasonably frank on an off-the-record basis. Media pressure on one has become intense. It's not just Cadoxton's death but the whole string of killings – a kind of constantly widening stain across the town.' As he spoke these last words it sounded for a second as if his calm might slip and hysteria take over. He fought back and won. 'That's what these editors and leader writers are saying. Purple stuff. I do think, though, that the public are unnerved by what's going on. This is legitimate concern and we must give some explanation. I'll take the chair. Obviously most of the talking and fielding of questions will fall to you.'

Oh, obviously.

'Some diabolical rumours about, you know,' Barton continued.

'Inevitable, sir.'

Iles said, 'It's a great pity you didn't have other officers with you in the Cadoxton business. The media don't understand how you come to be carrying out that kind of operation unsupported.'

'I don't understand myself,' Barton muttered.

'It could have been something or nothing,' Harpur told them. 'Calling out the cavalry might have looked like panic.'

Barton nodded. Panic stalked him daily and he had to approve every attempt to rout it.

Iles thought a press conference unwise and said so. Increasingly he would differ openly with Barton as the Chief neared retirement date and his power started to fade. 'One bloody thing Scargill is right about is journalism,' Iles said. 'Grinning, lying sods, longing to give us a good slagging.'

'We'll take them into our confidence – I mean to a small degree,' Barton replied. 'That makes them feel part of things, disarms them.'

'I know that's what the lectures at Bramshill say, sir. I'd put all the bastards on the other side of the wall.'

'It takes all sorts,' Barton adjudicated. 'Live and let live.'

Iles did a parody crossing of himself behind Barton's back and then held his hands to his chin as if in prayer. He had things about right, Harpur thought. The press turned his guts. But he, too, found a smile from somewhere to bring to the conference and keep prominent.

'I'd like to begin by saying we are not here,' Barton announced. 'And this meeting has not taken place. What you learn here you have learned by your own admirable methods elsewhere. Nothing is for quotation. In the event of comebacks, all will be denied. Now, Mr Harpur will take your questions.' Cop-outs had been named after this cop.

Harpur had intended giving them a short rundown confirming what he assumed they had already dug out for themselves. He would link the three deaths and the raid on Lloyd's as vaguely as he could without sounding inane or obstructive. When what he told them was printed, Holly would read it and imagine all the police forces in Britain must be dogging him. He might leave the country and the chance of settling with the bastard would be gone. Yet Harpur did not see how he could say less than this, and then answer a few questions – which would probably bring out a bit more. His job was to give as much or as little as would save the sensitive innards of the

Chief from what he called pressure.

There were five reporters, two for London papers, three local, all picked by Barton because they had done him favours in the past. Looking at them, Harpur suddenly had the conviction that they knew next to nothing. It showed in their faces and he was used to reading faces. In any case, couldn't you bet on it that the kind of reporters Barton selected would not have tried any troublesome digging? These five would be aware there had been murders and a bank raid, but he doubted whether they could see the links. Why tell the idle sods? Maybe that was what Barton wanted, to scare Holly out of sight and out of mind – say, down to Malaga where extradition still did not run and from where he could give the Chief and the town no more angst. Yes, that would be Barton's real purpose. Well, bugger him. Harpur abruptly decided only to take questions. Let these aces show what they had. He felt as sure as need be that it would not be much.

And he was right. They had discovered almost bugger-all for themselves. Because Cadoxton's death was the most recent they wanted to talk mainly about that, so Harpur in his replies gave a true-ish account of what had gone on at the killing, describing the Holly figure as unidentified, which was fair enough. Avery and the Pocket they talked about as entirely separate deaths, separate from Cadoxton and from each other. The local papers seemed worried about the number of dark incidents in the town but did not understand that they merged with each other into one engulfing black shadow. Harpur gave no enlightenment. Barton must have wanted more said, much more, but he did not offer anything. Could a Chief Constable publicly dish out confidential information beyond the wishes of his man on the case? When the conference was over he made the best of it and said, 'I think that will clear the air. It was a wise move. Always wise to be as open as possible. Within reason.'

Harpur could not pursue this juicy discussion because he was called away to return an urgent telephone call. No name had been left, but he recognized the number as a public booth he and Jack Lamb sometimes used.

'Problem, Col. I believe you know some of it. I've had a visit.'

'Christ, Holly?'

'No, no, not yet. Small fry.'

'Michael Martin Allen.'

'He says Holly wants the art and 100 grand in small bills to compensate or – But you'll be familiar with this.'

'Not the 100 Gs. He's upping.'

'Well, he can, can't he, now your bank man is gone?'

'Where's Allen?'

'In the car boot. One of the features of the Carlton, you know: they advertise you can get a slob in it. Don't worry, he's comfortable, and not badly damaged.'

'He came to your house?'

'Frightened Fay. My mother might have been there, Col. It won't do, not at all. It was like the bloody milkman calling for his money, as cool as cool. Why shouldn't they be, Col? Everything must look super-safe. Well, I'm going to work on him for Holly's address. Have to admit I've failed to find it.'

'I doubt whether he has it.' The number in the bottom of the match box had turned out to be a pay phone at White City. Even rag-tag-and-bobtail these days knew the basics of secure communications. 'Look, don't hurt him.'

'Who?'

'Allen. Or Holly – I mean, don't try it with Holly.'

'Isn't the bugger becoming too much?'

'We can deal with him in other ways.'

'Who can? Which other ways?'

Harpur thought, but could find no quick replies.

'Other ways?' Jack persisted. 'Sit-on-your-arse ways? Barton ways, Col? You've been institutionalized, you know. You're talking to the new spirit of Britain, individual enterprise. I sometimes think people like me are the only true risk-taking entrepreneurs who – '

'There aren't any people like you.'

' – who make their own way, settle their own problems, remove opposition.'

'If you knock shit out of Allen you could be institutionalized

142

for a long while yourself. And if you try it on with Holly on your own you could be one worse than institutionalized.'

'Partners then? I was thinking of asking you to help when I'm ready. He's messing both of us about, after all.'

'Well, I'll think about that – partnership.' What was there to think about, for God's sake? He and Lamb were partners already. And hadn't he reduced the Chief's treacherous press conference to nothing, to make sure Holly could be hit?

That night he found himself shoved even harder towards the vengeance trail and again it was on account of Ruth Avery. Somehow what happened to her got to him, even more strongly than threats to his daughter: maybe he found it hard to take seriously any threat that came via Allen, though that might turn out to be very stupid. They brought Mrs Avery in for drunkenness, and because of who she was did not charge her but told Harpur. He hurried from home and saw her in his office. By the time he arrived she had begun to sober up but was still pretty bad, her voice sharp and high and aggressive, her mind in and out of focus, her face askew. The change in her appearance was not just booze, though. Since he'd last seen her she seemed to have aged seven or eight years, and it shook him to note the difference. In a nice cheerful-looking way she had been too fat. Now the weight had dropped from her and she was gaunt and a little stooped, like someone sick.

'Ah, the chief of detectives,' she said, when Harpur came in. 'Now everything's going to be wonderful.'

'Ruth, they'll take you home in a little while. Nothing more will come of this.'

'*They'll* take me home? Why not you? Am I wrong or were you yearning for my treasure only a few weeks ago? So what's bloody happened? Where's the old sex drive?' She laboriously got up out of her chair, crossed the room and stood hard against him, drawing one hand up his thigh and into his crotch. 'Nice.' He took her back to her chair. 'Sorry,' she said. 'I'm not too bad now and then. That was then.'

'Are you eating properly?'

'Some love talk!'

He was afraid she would get up again and restart the mock-

143

ery of a seduction. To see her like this made him sad and angry once more. But she did not approach and instead seemed to go into a sudden spell of total clarity. 'I've been sticking at my inquiries, you know, trying to find who did Brian.'

'Yes?'

'This will seem pretty goofy to you, but I thought in my simple way that if he was washed up from the sea he might have been dropped in from a small boat. So I went and talked to people down at the estuary and the docks. It seemed – well, obvious.'

'Yes.'

'Have you been down there?'

'We're following other inquiries at the moment.'

'Yes? Well, you could be wise. I didn't find too much. A lot of hoofing and talking and taking back-chat for very little. An old, old man who sometimes sleeps on his boat is on deck late one night and sees two guys moving something heavy into one of the punts that can be hired down there. It's too far and too dark for him to be sure about anything – what it was or what they looked like. The people who hired out the punt can't remember too much about the man who took it, except that he was local with fair hair. There were two other people – men he thinks – in a car, waiting for him, a new car, but he doesn't know what make, and good clothes, not local. It was supposed to be fishing, of course.' She grew silent and yawned enormously.

Allen, Young, and Holly himself?

'No, you're probably right. It's a waste of time asking around down there – bits of nothing.'

She made him feel like the dud reporters Barton had invited to the conference, and for that Holly would eventually have to pay. Hard to recall now that this case had started out as a bank job, big but routine. Harpur had turned it into a duel, a conflict one-to-one between him and evil. Every policeman was warned off that grandiose play-acting, and before this case he had always been able to avoid it, telling his boys the job was a job, not a mission. After this he might not feel like giving that sermon again. Something that went so much further than the job said Holly had to be destroyed.

'A lot of the stuff you've found could turn out useful, Ruth – taken with everything else.'

'What's that then, the everything else?'

'We get information from all over.'

'What happens to it?'

'Well, it's processed.'

'Processed.' She made that sound the same as buried. Yes, this girl was clever.

'If it adds up, we act on it.'

'I hope so.' She stood. 'So, who's taking me home tonight?' Once more she yawned. 'Not you? That little fire hasn't died, has it?'

It hadn't, despite the changes in how she looked, but he said, 'I'll get a patrol to drop you off. I've a few things to do.'

'Like go home to your wife.'

That was one.

'You could say I was a merry widow, but not merry merry, pissed merry. It makes a difference, I suppose.' She tried to smooth down her clothes and patted her hair.

'Can I ask them to give you a meal before you go?'

'Thank you no, doc. I'll be fine.' She walked across the room to him and for a second he thought she was about to start fooling again. Instead, she shook his hand, 'I wouldn't be surprised to see us in touch, would you?'

'Not a bit.' Her prettiness would return once all this was settled.

'That's good, then.'

But the case seemed to have come to a stop, and for twenty-four hours Harpur had the feeling that all his chances were dead. His prayers had been shot down and the vengeance mission lay wrecked. The silence and emptiness and the guilt over his failures savaged him so that he could hardly think. Then things got suddenly a lot worse. Through the post he received a copy of the *Daily Express* in a wrapper, a signal that Lamb wanted to see him in the hypermarket car-park. It was not Lamb who turned up, though, but Fay, full of very big fears, and as soon as she spoke he understood why. 'Jack's gone away. He said you knew about it.'

At once he smelled catastrophe over the perfume. It was in Lamb's power to wipe out the lot – destroy himself and every chance for ever. 'Gone where?' He knew she could not answer.

'We had an arrangement. If he failed to telephone me in any period of twenty-four hours I was to get in touch with you.'

'OK, so you've done that, have you? What next?'

She was ashamed. 'It's over two days since I heard from him.'

'Christ!'

'I didn't want to, well, panic. You know what I mean?'

He would have liked to tear her to bits but said as quietly as he could, 'What was the arrangement, Fay? If he didn't make contact what were you supposed to tell me?'

She had on a capacious, multi-coloured, long cotton dress which eddied everywhere in her Maestro, swathing gear lever and brake and hiding most of the seat-belt in its folds. From somewhere underneath her she produced a blank, sealed envelope.

God, messages by letter! The hours of delay stretched out of sight. His control splintered. 'Couldn't you have phoned me?'

'Security. That wasn't the arrangement.'

She kept to bits of it, the stupid bits. In the envelope he found only a small piece of paper. The address of what seemed to be a farm near Sevenoaks in Kent was written there. Then came the words, '*Help me, pronto, partner.*' He did not show it to Fay but she obviously sensed it was a cry for help. Perhaps Mrs Lamb had been right after all to see symptoms of fear in Jack.

'Can you do anything for him, Col?'

'I'll leave now.'

He had a lot of driving to do. Thank God he was using a decent car these last few days while they spruced up another banger for him. At once he started back towards the station to draw a pistol again, met thick traffic, and gave up the idea. This was the time, more than any other, when he might need a gun but there had been too many delays already. Pulling out of the queue he did a U-turn across the street island and set out. He radioed Control to say he would be unreachable for a while on a surveillance job, then switched off.

He tried to prepare himself. As he saw things, Lamb had forced Holly's bolt-hole address from Michael Martin Allen and gone there to settle things, maybe taking Allen, maybe not. And Holly would have been ready for him, of course. This twat Lamb had done exactly what Harpur had warned him against and stuck his great, brainy head into a trap. The rural setting made things worse. It would be somewhere remote and short of witnesses. In the country no bugger thought anything of the sound of gunfire, but this time it would be the matter of a rabbit weighing just short of 18½ stone. Now, Holly might think the matter was nicely closed, could be there by himself or with a bird. It had to be Harpur's second chance, and after all the cock-ups he must take it.

He reached the area of the farm in mid-afternoon and left his car. It was as bad as he had feared. This place had been carefully chosen, with a main approach on a long, narrow dirt track between tall hedges. He could just make out part of the house frontage from the far end of the track, a few hundred yards off. Anything on wheels going in that way would be seen a good couple of minutes before arrival. He decided he could not even wait for darkness.

First, he tried to scout out another approach to the house from over fields and then rested for a couple of minutes in an old pillbox from the war, where he armed himself with a half house-brick: didn't everyone say the police had moved in on new technology? It would do at least as well as a Leica. What kind of system was it when police brass could not carry a piece as standard when there might be a shooting? All that fucking form-filling and signing – Christ, you could prove a will easier. But that was the way things operated, and he had to wear it; until this case had been content to wear it. Not now, and bugger what the new guide-lines said. He felt he was growing up.

When he moved, he went fast. For all he knew he might

have been spotted and someone could be coming to find him. On the early part of the approach he could give himself fair cover by sticking close to the hedges. His backwoodsman training stopped there. The first field sloped up, and when he came to the end of it he found himself looking down on the house and out-buildings with a passable view of the back and one side. He saw no vehicles, but from the house came the kind of heavy beat Radio 1 music his children would have listened to all day if there hadn't been thicker drivel on television. He took off again, worried about dogs, worried about shotguns, worried about the music because it meant there would be no listening for the enemy.

He entered a second field and began the last stage of his approach, down the slope this time and no longer in the comforting shadow of the hedge. Madness to try this in daylight, and bigger madness to lose any more time. He had picked out the rear door which he would try first. If it was open, it might be an invitation to walk into a welcome; if it wasn't, he would have to do what he could on the lock, making no sound and using only his bunch of passkeys, which sometimes struck lucky and sometimes didn't – this was a long way from the Ernest Bevin and universal access.

He ran. At least their muck music would blot out the noise of his feet on the pebbles.

But as he sprinted, the din cut off abruptly and the silence appalled him. He felt as if he had suddenly been picked up by a searchlight, pinpointed, a target, and he gripped the half house-brick so frantically that its surface crumbled and pieces dug into his skin. Had he been spotted? Where was Holly watching him from?

Harpur had reached the door but thought about pulling back, right back, across the fields again, into his car and away. He should get help. The urge to do it all solo, to clean up on the glory and let the blood-lust loose, was pushing him into lunatic risks and for a moment he saw them all in terrible clarity. Some panic impulse told him to get out fast from a spot that had always been shitty and was now super-shitty. Nothing in a partnership said one member had to get killed the same way as the other. What partnership, anyway, for God's sake? Was he his grass's keeper, even Jack Lamb? Fear had him by the scruff like a hawk on a mouse.

All the same he hung on, partly because he did not trust his legs, partly because he dreaded being out in the open again, under a bright sun, scuttling for cover. Cowering against the door seemed to give some small shelter. Over the years he had learned a bit about fear and panic. They came to him from time to time and blotted out his brain for a moment or two, but if he could keep still just briefly the worst would go and he would be capable of something again. These fits could happen to anyone; something absurd could set them off. Today it had been the sudden loss of the music that had knocked him sideways. Silence broke him up. Crazy.

Putting down the brick for a second he pulled on gloves. Then he tried the door. It opened, and he waited, standing to the side of the opening with the house-brick cocked, waiting for Holly to make his move. Harpur was recovering and his mind had started working again, though not on top form yet. He was acting as if Holly might come rushing out to grab him, whereas all he needed to do was wait until Harpur put himself in that door frame and then blow his middle out, a trespasser.

Brick ready, he entered very fast and swung the door back, shutting it without too much sound. Immediately he went flat and listened again, hearing nothing. In a while he got on his hands and knees and edged a few yards forward. He was in a kind of scullery and saw another closed door opposite, up a couple of steps, which must lead to the kitchen proper or a living-room. Rising to his feet he moved to this door, put his ear to it and tried to quieten his breathing. After a few seconds he went through the opening drill again.

Beyond was a kitchen-cum-dining-area and it had been totally wrecked. In his time he had seen five hundred houses in this sort of mess, and for a second he thought there had been a burglary. This was not work of thieves or vandals, though. No drawers or cupboards were open, no contents spilled. The devastation was broken furniture, smashed ornaments and pictures, and a wide bloodstain down one wall, as if someone badly hurt had taken support from it and then crashed to the floor. A couch in gold velvet had been snapped across the middle and sagged to the ground. Nearby stood a shattered dining-chair. He picked his way about the room, trying to read the signs of what had happened here.

In a way it all reminded him of that William Walton Avenue fortress, but there was one crucial difference: in that place he had realized early on that nobody remained, but here his instincts told him very strongly that someone else was present. He had heard nothing, seen nothing, to make him think so, yet he knew it to be true. Holly was in what must be the main lounge at the front, or upstairs, waiting for Harpur to come looking. It was Holly who had stopped the music so he could chart the steps of Harpur's approach.

He passed into the front hallway. Destruction continued there, and he found more blood on the wall and smearing a green telephone and the round table it stood on. Large sliding doors, partly open, led to the lounge at the front, and through the gap he could see a small revolving bookcase and a framed county print on the wall. Now, from somewhere to the right in that room, there came the sudden sound of movement. It was slight and not repeated, but was unmistakable and Harpur reacted at once. He expected Holly to appear armed and ready between the doors, and took a couple of quick steps to put himself alongside the opening. Once more he raised the brick, poised to crash it down as soon as Holly showed. It would have to be one single effective blow or Holly would have the chance to use his armament and Harpur was finished.

For perhaps two minutes he waited, his hand with the brick in it high over his head. There was still no repetition of the sound. Harpur suddenly came to fear that Holly might have left the lounge by the window and would come up on him from the front or back of the house. He was a sucker here, like someone miming a tennis serve. With his free hand he felt for the knob on the sliding door, held it briefly while he prepared himself, then dragged the door open and hurtled into the room, swinging the brick and screaming, 'Police! Stand still! This is a raid!' Anything to make him sound like a battalion.

150

He had it right: the house was not empty. Under a rosewood table Michael Martin Allen lay facing the doors, his fair hair matted with blood and hanging down over his forehead, no longer built into that winning quiff. Harpur rapidly surveyed the rest of the room, but there was nobody else. He approached Allen and crouched so that their faces were close. This man was near death. That sound of movement must have been a tiny last shift of position, or perhaps the final spasm of his muscles. Allen's eyes were open but they registered nothing, not when Harpur spoke his name nor even when he touched his shoulder. It was not the brown suit and felt pretty good. He must have been spending.

While Harpur was crouched close like Florence Nightingale there came a sudden sharp sound from the other side of the lounge. He threw up an arm to protect his head and turned quickly: Christ, had he taken the bait himself? Here he was, bent down, last-riting, unprotected, half-dazed by the sight of Allen, a sitter. He had walked into it, as much a sucker as Jack Lamb. Yet no blow came, and no bullet. In a moment, though, the foul music suddenly blasted out again. He raised his head a little further and saw the sharp sound had been a timing device switching on. Someone here had been bothered about intruders and someone had been right.

Quickly Harpur went through the rest of the house. Certain that for now, at least, he was not menaced, he put the brick on the ground and did some random pull-outs of drawers. In a desk he found papers in the name of Mr Ronald Western, and a couple of envelopes containing invitations and an advertising brochure addressed to Angela Barclay. Was Holly 'Ron Western' in the country, and was Angela his out-of-town solace? Did it matter? He knew what had happened and could do nothing about it, not even report what he had found. He had no right to be in this house and no proper explanation for his conduct, nothing that he could put to Barton or the local police, especially with Allen lying there. It was mad to hang about. He might have been spotted by some neighbour on the way across the fields or parking his car. Farmers sat on a lot of loot and would be ever-ready to dial the police for help if they saw something shady.

Before leaving he looked once more at Allen and discovered he was now unquestionably dead. Far beyond questions. Harpur searched him and found nothing in his pockets but a little money. Yes, he must have learned fast about security – not that it had done him much good.

It looked as if Holly had seen off Lamb, then taken the body somewhere for disposal. The grief Harpur felt went double-deep because nothing had been accomplished here either by Jack or himself. He tried again to visualize what had gone on. Perhaps Allen had helped Holly, and been shot in the fight. Holly might come back to help him, or even to dispose of him, if he had realized Allen could not live. But Harpur saw another possibility as much more likely: Holly might simply disappear for a long spell. Had the time come for Mr Ronald Western to move on? To wait here in the hope that he might return would be lunatic even by the obsessed standards Harpur had been following lately. It could be for ever.

One day there might be a third chance for him, but it was not here.

19

Some magic had been worked on Barton. When Harpur was next called to see him, the Chief seemed suddenly to have shed his lethargy and aura of eternal pain. Iles also looked chirpy. The Chief's smile was no longer that one which said he would gamely take whatever came from a bloody-minded fate, but a fuller, almost gurgling display, a smile of raw triumph. 'Col, this is between the three of us at the moment, understood? I've had an Assistant Chief acquaintance of mine on from Kent. I was talking with him about some of our problems at the last Chief Officers' shindig, so he knows where my interests lie. He tells me that the body of a white male has been recovered from the sea near Margate overnight. The man does not appear to have drowned but died from gunshot wounds. The body was unclothed so definite identification is taking a little time but – '

'What kind of physique?' Harpur blurted. 'How big?'

'Big? Why? I'm not sure he gave me that. But, look, they're pretty sure this is Rex Holly.'

'Who are you thinking of, Col?' Iles asked.

Barton went on, 'They know Holly pretty well in Kent, apparently. He has a farmhouse where he lives part of the time under alias. They had him spotted as soon as he moved in, of course. He gives no trouble, so they've had to put up with him. They're getting a woman friend to look at the body but they're not in any real doubt.'

Harpur found himself almost giggling with surprise and relief.

'You were expecting something like this, but not quite like this, Col?' Iles asked.

'No, no. How did it happen, though?'

'They're working on it,' Barton said. 'Gangland fracas? There's another unknown dead involved, not in the sea, but connected somehow.' His smile widened. 'Who says there is no God? Hasn't He tidied this one up for us sweetly? For all sorts of excellent reasons, we did not want to tangle directly with Holly, despite what we knew and suspected; and it looked as if he had dodged us, made fools of us. Who's the fool now, though – washed up at a place like bloody Margate?' He snorted and chuckled. 'So fish-and-chippy! It was bound to happen, I suppose, with a grasping sod like Holly. They've been out to his place at Sevenoaks and found signs of a top-class battle. That's where the second corpse was. The woman who usually ministers to him there was away in London or she might have got it, too, and ID would have been even tougher. Thank God that, as police officers, there will always be instances where we can just sit back, not burn our fingers or soil our clothes, and let these bastards do our work for us, knocking hell out of each other.' He nodded and chuckled again. 'This will just about close the book, won't it? Oh, I know Colin and Francis Garland have to do their bit over Leo Peters' death with the inquiry, but I've had a word with the

ACC handling that, and he foresees no problems.

Iles said, 'Looking at you, Col, I still have the impression that you're harbouring a few ideas of your own about all this?'

'No, like the Chief's,' Harpur said, after hesitation meant to signify thought. 'Gang war. Someone's knocking off someone's floozie or – '

Barton's phone rang and he held up a hand for silence.

'Donald, good of you to call again so soon.' He began to make more notes, occasionally repeating some of the words he was hearing for Iles and Harpur. 'Positively identified as Holly. Fingerprints as well as the woman, Barclay. Fine. Yes. In the water three hours. Good. That's time for a nice cleansing soak, isn't it? Second man shot with a Mauser belonging to Holly and found at the house. Fascinating. Have we ID on this second character? Not yet. Not a local villain but you can't say more. Excellent, Donald. I hope we can do something for you one day. Yes, very hard on Barclay, poor slut. Traces of face wounds on Holly, besides the fatal shot. Possibly a glassing. What vigorous lives these people have. How do they survive? No, quite so, they don't, do they?'

By early afternoon they had identified Allen, and Iles called Harpur in to tell him. 'Did you have an idea along these lines, Col?'

'Allen? How the hell could I? What's he doing in *Kent*, for God's sake?'

Iles gazed at him.

'Do we need to notify anyone?' Harpur said.

'We've been out to his place on the Ernest Bevin. Somebody calling herself Mrs Allen was there.'

All those clothes in the wardrobe did have an owner, then.

'We told her. She listened, and shut the door.'

'Par for the Ernest Bevin.'

When he was driving home that evening Lamb's Carlton passed him, and from the passenger seat Fay waved excitedly through the window and indicated that he should follow them. They pulled up a little further on at the church of St Mark, decorated with a banner advertising *Grand Summer Jumble Sale in aid of the Roof Fund*. By the time Harpur arrived, Jack and Fay were already inside and he found them at the women's clothes counter, Fay delightedly sorting through dresses. Jack and he wandered off to the Odds and Bobs. 'Never know what you'll find in these dos,' Jack said, handling some repellent metal brooches.

'It's no time ago that I was at a market with Rex Holly. Vivid life in the police.'

'Did you like your little trip to the Garden of England?'

'Where were you?'

'Not far off. I wanted you to see for yourself.'

'See what?'

'See and – see and get involved. A partnership where one member does all the work is no good.' No, Mrs Lamb was wrong about him. Jack had all his old confidence. Harpur was glad.

'Why kill poor old Allen?'

'Not me, Col. Look, Allen coughed the address and I took him along, hostage, shield, guide. I would have let the bugger go eventually, but I couldn't have him sending out warnings in advance, could I? So, we arrive in the farmhouse and Holly starts popping off right away – I didn't blame him. Allen got hit at once. Me, a bit luckier, a bit cleverer. Well, of course. Then I had to reply. One bullet was all it took to do Holly, Col. I'm pleased with that. Well, Allen was dying, so I left him. I thought I'd put Holly in the sea, just to round things off. No real need, but it seemed a match for what they did to your man Avery.'

Fay called. She was holding some huge, flouncy creation in a dazzling range of colours against her, and beaming. Lamb beamed back and silently clapped in acknowledgement of her taste.

'Allen, yes,' Lamb went on. 'Good job I had him with me, you know. I'm not sure whether Holly was shooting at him or me. Maybe he thought Allen had gone over. Anyway, it was

Allen he hit.'

'I left a half house-brick at the place. It will have my dabs on it.'

'You're not on record, are you, Col? Don't fret. I went back afterwards, just in case Allen could do with a doctor. I got rid of the brick. Thought it looked your style.' Fay was coming to rejoin them. 'Must get together soon, Colin, formally. I've heard something that could be up your street.'

'Oh, lovely,' Fay cried, seeing the brooches. 'Is Mark the patron saint of collectors?'

Harpur left. He had been drawn much deeper into this strange and abiding relationship with Jack, drawn in as deep as complicity in a killing. And Lamb had deliberately brought it about, 'involved' him, as he put it. Lamb was even bigger and rougher and more capable than he had seemed before. In a way it worried Harpur, but not too much. He could understand why Lamb should want to reinforce the bonds, make Harpur safe by pulling him right into the dirt. It was how narking worked, and always had. If a cop couldn't walk that tightrope, he ought to try some other game. He had always known that, just as he had always known there were times when 'Shoot first' was the only real policy. Now he knew both better.

Next day Holly's death made the front pages, and during the twenty-four hours that followed Harpur had two strange messages. A couple of people he valued thought he had lived up to his boasting and done what was required with Holly and he decided not to correct the mistakes, at least not yet. First, Ruth Avery telephoned him at home, sober and hearty. 'Good boy, Colin. I knew you'd do it. Brian would be proud of you.'

'We ought to talk these things over.'

'Why not?'

'Soon.'

'Why not?'

There was also a handwritten note in green ink. It came on the letter-headed paper of the black preacher he had met at Royston Paine's funeral. Anstruther wrote: 'Vengeance may

156

be the Lord's but He can sometimes do with a little aid. This was high and noble achievement, officer. Mrs Paine says thanks, the boy Grenville says thanks. I say thanks, and God bless you.'